BIGFOOT ATTACK
ERIC S. BROWN

SEVERED PRESS

BIGFOOT ATTACK

BIGFOOT ATTACK!

It had taken almost the entire day to finish their hike up into the hills that surrounded Canton, North Carolina. The slopes were steep and far from easy going. Danny rubbed at his thighs sitting in the deer blind they'd stumbled onto. The structure was old but stable. He'd been willing to risk climbing into it for the view it provided of the large clearing to the west. To the north, south, and east were the typical woods native to the region. A quick scan of the area with their thermal imaging, remote control helicopter hadn't turned up anything before the sun set but Danny knew in his gut that the monster they were after was up here somewhere.

His crew consisted of himself, Layton, Riley, and Joe. Layton was the group's real tracker, a gruff older man who was always armed to the teeth. Riley was their tech. Joe was, no offense to the guy, their grunt labor and far from the sharpest tool in the shed. The four of them had been together, chasing monsters in the woods, for a couple of years now when time and money allowed them to.

Tonight, they were spread out as usual with Layton prowling the woods, alone, while Joe and

Riley kept back down the hill below the clearing a decent ways, watching through the scattered cameras they had managed to get set up before nightfall. Danny had his eyes on the woods as well from his spot in the rickety old deer blind, taking turns between using the thermal imaging of his phone and the night vision goggles that were presently shoved up onto his forehead.

Thus far, the night had been a drag, uneventful and utterly boring. Danny stole a glance at his watch. It was shortly past midnight now. They were in the real thick of the night but he was thankful the weather was clear. Darkness could be dealt with a lot better than rain when they were on the hunt.

They came to this region because of the local legends. Those stories were too numerous to be discounted. Some of them were very recent as well. They gave Danny hope that tonight would be the night. Somewhere in these hills was supposedly a beast that walked on two legs like a man and he was determined to find it.

Every member of the crew carried a handheld radio except for Layton who wore a military grade headset. They were only to be used for emergencies or more vital situations but Danny had to admit to himself that not even he always stuck with that intent. His radio sat next to him inside the deer blind, tempting him to pick it up and ask how the others were doing though he knew they would have contacted him already if anything interesting had come their way.

Danny nearly leapt to his feet as the radio crackled to life, startling the hell out of him. The sudden shifting of his weight made the deer blind shake beneath him, its wood creaking loudly. The blind held though. The floor didn't give out from under Danny nor did the aged stand go toppling over.   Bracing himself, Danny regained his balance as Riley's voice came through the radio. Riley wasn't screaming but it was easy to hear the amount of effort being put into keeping his voice quiet.

"We got movement down here!" Riley said. "And I ain't fooling around! It really looks like. . ."

The radio crackled, cutting out briefly. When it cleared, Riley was still talking.

"You guys need to get here A.S.A.P," Riley laughed. "You're missing out! If it keeps coming, we'll have honest to God eyes on it soon!"

"Holy!" Danny heard Joe cry out in the background through Riley's radio. His shout wasn't like Riley's. There was fear in it.

"Oh God, please. . ." Riley suddenly blurted out. "Danny! You gotta. . ."

And then, the radio went silent.

Danny clicked his radio on. "Riley! Riley, come in. What's going on down there?"

The answer he got was a sharp crackle of static.

"Danny! Joe! Come in!" Danny shouted. "Answer me, damn it!"

"Stop wasting your breath, man," Layton's voice came over the radio. "They're not going to answer you."

"Layton?" Danny stammered, shocked by the older man cutting in. Layton pretty much never broke radio silence.

"I'm on my way to them, Danny," Layton told him. "I need you stay where you are until you hear different. You copy?"

Danny wanted to tell the old man to go to hell and that he was about to start down towards where Riley and Joe were sat, but didn't. The old man was seldom wrong and right now, Layton was taking what actions he thought were needed to keep them all as safe as possible. Rationally, Danny knew that but it was difficult to accept it emotionally. His concern for Riley and Joe was deep and sincere. The stories about the creature in this region. . . they weren't like the ones out west. This thing in these hills, according to the locals, would attack and even kill those who violated its turf sometimes. And he was the one who had led them into these woods; if something did happen to Riley and Joe, it was on him.

"Danny," Layton called out, "I need you to

tell me that you still have the gun I gave you."

"I do," Danny answered, shivering in the night air from the sweat that now slicked his skin.

"Get it out and get it ready, Danny," Layton ordered him.

"Do you think. . .?" Danny asked.

"I don't know yet," Layton barked. "Just be ready in case."

"Will do," Danny assured the old man.

Keeping a tight hold on the radio, Danny moved to where he'd sat his backpack and began digging through its contents in search of the weapon Layton had reminded him of. Danny hated guns. He'd never owned one. Carrying one on this trip . . . well, Layton had pretty much forced that one on him. His fingers found and closed around the butt of the pistol. Danny pulled it out of his backpack and sat staring at the weapon. Its cool metal gleamed in the light of the stars that crept into the deer blind. With a sigh, Danny readied the gun, his thoughts drifting back to Layton. If Riley and Joe were truly in trouble, Layton should be reaching them soon. That brought him some comfort at least. The old man didn't screw around and he was packing some serious firepower if needs must.

The booming crack of a distant rifle shot rang out in the night. Danny jerked at the sound of it, shaking the blind again. He knew it was time to get down out of it. As quickly as he could while still being careful, Danny snatched up his pack and began climbing down out of the blind. He dropped the last few feet from the dry rotting ladder onto the ground as another shot cracked in the distance. This time it was followed by two more in rapid succession.

Danny clicked on his radio. "Layton! What the hell is going on out there?"

There was no answer from the old man and no more gunshots either. The night was still and quiet once more. Danny wiped sweat from where it beaded on his forehead with the backside of his hand and shivered. He felt sick. Danny had spent most of his life chasing monsters but never in all those years did he ever think finding one would go down like tonight was. He'd never imagined that it could happen like this, with his people in danger.

Danny tried to tell himself that it was all just some kind of mix up, that there was no danger. Maybe the other guys were just messing with him. As much as he wanted to believe those lies, he couldn't. The sound of the rifle shots had damningly told the truth of things. He stood below the deer blind for a moment, trying to get himself together. What the hell was he supposed to do now? If Layton was in trouble too then whatever was happening had to be way beyond his skillset. Nonetheless, Danny knew he couldn't just make a run for it. Those people out there were his friends, his best friends. Hell, they were his family. He had to try find to out what was going on, help them somehow.

The woods were dark but the night was clear. The moon and stars lit his way as Danny hurried down towards Riley and Joe's position that was the group's base camp. With each step, his pace grew faster and faster. Danny couldn't control the fear within him anymore. He sucked breath into his lungs in ragged gasps as his legs pumped beneath him.

He heard the thing coming in his direction. Limbs snapped, wood splintering and breaking in its path as the massive creature barreled its way towards him. Danny stopped in his tracks, staring at the approaching horror. The beast stood over eight feet tall, all hair and primal rage. Its arms and legs were so thickly muscled, Danny could see them rippling beneath the thing's filthy, brown hair that covered its body, head to toe. Yellow eyes with an almost supernatural glow burned in the darkness as the beast let out a roar that seemed as loud as a crash of thunder.

Danny swung his pistol up, aiming its barrel at the beast. His hands were trembling as he squeezed the weapon's trigger. The pistol's unexpected recoil almost caused him to drop it.

Danny couldn't remember the last time he'd fired a gun and he was paying for that now. Despite the beast's size and its growing proximity, he missed. The bullet he fired hammered into the low-lying limb of a tree between him and the beast. That limb was shattered into bits of wood mere seconds later as the beast plowed through it.

He fired again at nearly point blank range. This time his shot hit the beast, striking the center of its chest. Blood splattered out from where the bullet pierced flesh but Danny could see that the beast's thick muscles stopped it from doing any real damage. Without anything more than a grunt of pain, the beast kept coming, not even slowed in the slightest by his effort to stop it. A huge, hair-covered hand lashed out, knocking the pistol from his grasp. The weapon spun away through the air as the beast's other hand shot forward, its fingers closing around his neck. Danny felt the heat of its body through the creature's hair as he heard the sharp crack of his own neck breaking under the pressure of its grip.

****

"Holy mother," Sheriff Bernard muttered, turning his face away from the savaged corpse inside the partially open body bag. It wasn't the stench of rot that sickened him but rather what he had seen. The man in the bag. . . half his face was gone, where skin had once been there was only the white of scraped and jagged, broken bone. The wound didn't look to have been inflicted by any kind of weapon that Sheriff Bernard could think of. It looked more like the work of an animal's claws.

Bernard stood up from where he knelt over the body bag and took a step back. "Close it up!" he ordered.

"Yes sir," a young paramedic nodded, zipping the bag shut.

"You think that's bad, wait until you see the other guys," Clarkson warned.

Bernard grunted. "Any idea what happened up there?"

Clarkson spat out a mouthful of tobacco juice and wiped at his lips then shook his head. "Not a freaking clue, boss man. . . not one that makes sense anyway. Best if you see it all for yourself, I think."

Around them at the end of the gravel road which led up the mountain there were most of his department's patrol cars and four of the county's ambulances. Quite a few still had their siren lights on, not that they were needed up here on the mountain in the daylight. Bernard figured it was just habit to have them on or ingrained training to do so perhaps.

"You coming?" Clarkson asked, heading into

the woods.

"Yeah," Bernard answered, his voice gruff, lips curled downward in a deep frown.

The two of them walked at an unhurried pace as Clarkson continued to chew on his tobacco. Bernard caved into his own craving, lighting up a cigarette.

"Those things will kill you," Clarkson snorted.

"Like you have room to talk," Bernard chuckled.

A moment passed in silence before Bernard asked, "So where exactly are we headed?"

"That poor bastard you saw in the body bag and his buddies were apparently some kind of crypto-folks. . ." Clarkson said.

"Cryptozoologists," Bernard corrected him.

"Yep. That sounds right," Clarkson nodded. "Anyway, they set up a base camp of sorts not far up ahead with two of their group manning it. Looks like whatever went down happened there first. The other two were further up the mountain and seemingly rushing down it when they got theirs."

Bernard knew Clarkson well enough to know that there was something the deputy was holding back. "Okay, what is it you're not telling me?"

"The two who weren't at the camp were armed," Clarkson told him. "One of them to the freaking teeth. That guy got off several shots too before he was taken out. Found the shell casings."

"And the other one?" Bernard asked.

"Just had a pistol," Clarkson shrugged. "Didn't appear to know how to use it well either."

"What makes you say that?" Bernard gave the gray-haired deputy a questioning look.

"I checked out his pistol already," Clarkson shook his head. "Fired two shots. One of them hit a tree a few yards from where he was sprawled out."

Clarkson spat out another mouthful of tobacco juice. "Neither of them made it to the camp."

The woods opened into a clearing. Sheriff Bernard was dang sure he didn't want to see what was in it but entered it anyway. Shattered equipment was all over the place. Bits of laptops, monitors, and cameras littered the ground. Thankfully, he discovered, the bodies had already been hauled down the mountain. Even so, from the amount of blood that stained the area, it was easy to see a massacre had taken place in the clearing.

"The two guys who were here died pretty quick," Clarkson said. "Whatever hit them did it fast and hard. Never stood a chance. They were torn to pieces and. . ."

Bernard waited for Clarkson to go on.

"Something took some bites out of them,"

Clarkson finished.

"You mean something was eating them?" Bernard's eyes narrowed.

"That's what it looks like to me," Clarkson said. "Waller can tell us for sure."

Waller was the county coroner. He was more than a touch odd but did his job well enough. Bernard never had any issues with his work, and was willing to endure Waller's eccentricity because of its quality.

"What about all this?" Bernard kicked a piece of broken laptop.

"Haven't found anything intact enough to look worth retrieving but don't worry, we'll send it all to Johnson and see what he can get out of them," Clarkson assured him.

Sheriff Bernard grunted and began taking his own look around the clearing. Deputy Clarkson had been up here before, he hadn't. Bernard took it all in as best he could. Clarkson gave him space and let him do what he needed to do.

"You ain't kidding," Sheriff Bernard sighed. "This is some real messed up crap."

"You saw the footprints then?" Clarkson asked.

"Wish I hadn't," Bernard frowned. "Get casts made of them A.S.A.P. I want them out to an expert before the end of the day."

"Copy that," Clarkson nodded. "I've never seen anything like them."

"Me either," Bernard concurred.

"You don't think that. . ." Clarkson let his words trail off, not voicing fully what he was thinking as if doing so might make those thoughts real or at the very least him seem like a raving lunatic. "Let's not jump to any conclusions," Bernard urged. "Let Waller and Johnson do their work. We can go from there. In the meantime, didn't you say there was another body that hadn't been taken down yet?"

"Yep," Clarkson pointed up the mountain. "It's up a ways yet. Not that I'd really call it a body anymore."

"Well, lead on then," Bernard ordered.

Deputy Clarkson started on up the mountain. Bernard followed him, his eyes scanning the trees as they went. He had to wonder if whatever killed the four men from the camp was still in the area. Everything he'd seen so far was pointing towards this being some sort of animal attack. Even the strange footprints could be explained away, he hoped, if the right experts took a gander at things. He'd heard of tracks that looked human-ish before but weren't.

Bernard felt as if there was something among the trees watching them as they continued their march to where the last body was still waiting for them. It was a feeling he couldn't shake. If it was an animal though, the thing was likely long gone. All the activity from his deputies and the paramedics in the area surely would have driven it away. That's what he wanted to believe but then again, whatever was up here had come at and killed four grown men apparently without much effort and then went on to make a meal out of them.

Coming to a stop ahead of him, Deputy Clarkson stepped aside so that he could come to stand beside him, saying, "This bastard got the worst of it."

The man, or rather what was left of him, was scattered all over the ground. It was as if something huge had torn him apart, a piece at a time. Bernard moved to take a better look at the closest of them, squatting down. It was one of the poor bastard's arms. His stomach groaned as a wave of sickness washed over him but Bernard fought it back. Something had gnawed on the arm as if it were a chicken leg. The teeth marks were easy to see in the small bits of meat that remained.

"God Almighty, have mercy," Bernard croaked and stood up again.

"Don't think God had anything to do with this mess up here, Sheriff," Clarkson snorted.

Bernard shot the deputy an angry glare.

Clarkson sniffed loudly, clearing his nose, and said, "I didn't want this moved until you could get a look at it."

"Now I've seen it, Clarkson," Bernard said,

keeping his voice as calm as he could. "Just make sure to remind the boys in the ambulances that this is evidence, okay?"

"Roger that," Clarkson nodded.

Animal attacks happened in places like this. The Lord knew that Bernard had dealt with his share of them but never anything like this. Not even close.

The sound of a twig snapping caused both him and Clarkson to jerk around. Bernard's .44 Magnum cleared its holster, drawn with the speed and skill of an Old West gunfighter. Clarkson's weapon came up a bit slower but was in the deputy's hand by the time he'd finished whipping around in the direction of the sound.

"Whoa!" A man cried out, his hands thrust upwards above his head.

"Paul!" Sheriff Bernard yelled. "What the hell are you doing up here?"

"You just came damn close to getting your ass shot off, son," Clarkson growled, lowering his weapon.

For his part, Paul was as freaked out by nearly being shot as they were over almost doing it.

"It's my job!" Paul blurted out. "I go where the trouble is."

"You work for the Canton Gazette, Paul," Clarkson mocked him. "Ain't much trouble except bar fights, accidents, and cats in trees around here."

"Yeah?" Paul challenged him. "Then what do you call. . ."

Paul's words came to an abrupt stop as he saw the human remains past where Bernard and Clarkson were standing. His face went a sickly shade of green as the small town journalist doubled over and vomited up his breakfast. Eggs, pancakes, and bacon from the look of it. The vomit splattered loudly onto the grass at Paul's feet.

"Mother fragger," Clarkson covered his mouth and nose at the smell of it.

Bernard wondered how a bit of vomit could bother the jaded deputy so much after everything else they'd seen that morning.

When Paul's heaving stopped, Bernard walked over to him, steadying the journalist, as he straightened up.

"You shouldn't be up here, Paul," Bernard told him.

"But. . ." Paul began to protest weakly.

"But nothing," Bernard said firmly. "We don't know what's happened here fully ourselves yet or if the danger's over. Whatever did that to the guy over there, Paul. . . it could still be up here with us."

"Oh crap," Paul muttered as Bernard felt the young man shudder through the grip he had on his shoulder. "Are you serious?"

"Deadly," Bernard assured him.

Paul started dry heaving again. Bernard let go of him, backing away, just in case anything else came out.

"Get it together, kid," Clarkson roared, frustrated and done putting up with Paul's crap. "We'll see you back down the mountain."

****

Just outside of town, five bikes raced along Old Marks Road. Brently was in the lead, something that no one saw coming. Warren and Pete were pushing themselves hard trying to catch up to the chubby kid on the downhill slope. Robbie and Megan were holding back, laughing at the others.

Brently squeezed his brakes, his bike skidding to a halt as he reached the battered wire fence which surrounded the abandoned farmhouse their crew used as a hang out. Warren nearly barreled into him, not able to stop as quickly.

"Watch it!" Warren shouted, as he jerked the handlebars of his bike to steer past Brently.

Pete, Robbie, and Megan rolled up behind them.

"I won, suckers!" Brently yelled out in triumph. "Y'all owe me a freaking pizza!"

Such a display was out of character for Brently who was usually calm and softly spoken but the excitement of actually winning for once appeared to give him an entirely different persona in the moment.

Warren dug into the pocket of his jeans, producing a handful of wadded up bills, and slapped them into Brently's hand.

Brently turned on the seat of his bike, looking at the others.

With a sigh, Pete slapped what cash he had into the chubby kid's hand too.

"Well?" Brently said to Megan and Robbie.

Megan laughed, shaking her head. "Uh-uh, buddy. That was between you guys."

"What she said," Robbie nodded, grinning.

"Fine," Brently sighed.

"I can't believe you won," Pete commented as Brently tucked his newly acquired cash away.

"Me either," Brently smiled. "Guess everyone gets lucky eventually."

"It wasn't luck," Warren was still scowling at his defeat. "It was mass and gravity!"

"Hey man!" Pete snapped at Warren, getting off his bike.

"It's okay," Brently held a hand towards Pete. "Really."

"So, guys. . ." Robbie spoke up unexpectedly. "You do know we're losing daylight."

It was true. They had a lot to do today. The summer was coming to an end. For everyone but Robbie that meant senior year was just around the corner. He'd dropped out the year before. None of the others held it against him.

They all still accepted him as part of the group. He knew Pete, Megan, and Brently felt bad for him though they would never tell him that to his face. And Warren, well, like with most things, he didn't give a crap.

Pete was the newest member of the group, having only joined up about a year ago. Robbie liked him. Pete had a good heart and a decent head on his shoulders. Even Warren was accepting of Pete which said a lot about what kind of guy he was. Despite his character, Pete was an oddity for their group. He was buff like a weightlifter, handsome with shaggy, sandy blonde hair, and deep blue eyes. The rest of them aside from Megan were geeks and nerds. Oh, she was just as smart as they were but Megan didn't look the part. Her skin was tan, hair midnight black, and with curves that, in the words of Mick Jagger, would "make a grown man cry". Warren and Brently had lusted after her for years but Robbie at least told himself that he wasn't like them, that he could put her looks aside. In truth, now, she was almost like a sister to him.

Robbie flinched as a rock bounced off his shoulder, snapping him out of his thoughts.

"Ow! What the heck, man?" Robbie looked at Warren, who was smirking, and trying to hold in his laughter. "What did you do that for?"

"You said to hurry up and then froze, A hole,"

Warren answered honestly and opened the rusty gate that led into the old farmhouse's yard. "You coming or not?"

Robbie felt like punching Warren in the face. After all these years, Warren still knew exactly how to tick him off. Megan must have somehow sensed what he was thinking because Robbie felt her hand on his shoulder. He sighed. She didn't even have to say anything. Just her touch was enough to remind him what he was thinking was wrong. However annoying Warren might be, he was their friend and part of the group.

The farmhouse looked like crap. Weeds grew up its walls and half its windows were shattered. The yard was overgrown, having not been mowed in a decade or more, it was like a jungle of tall grass. None of that mattered to them though. They didn't come to this place for its beauty.

The house's interior was just as nasty as it was outside with some spots in the floor so rotted that they weren't safe anymore. Its basement. . . well, that was another story. They had fixed it up and turned it into a base of operations and storage room for their group. Brently had even rigged them up a solar battery outside and rewired the basement so that it had power.

Warren made it across the lawn first and swung up the hatch-like door to the basement.

The others were right on his heels. None of them planned on actually hanging out in the revamped basement today. They just needed some of their gear and then it would be time to hit the woods.

Robbie remembered how their group got started. All of them, except maybe Pete, at least claimed to believe that the stories of a monster that prowled the woods around and above Canton were real. Brently just loved crypto-myths. Any chance to track a monster in real life was enough to get him excited. Warren, though he rarely spoke of it these days, had told them back then that he thought the monster was responsible for the death of his father. Megan was the only one in the group who claimed to have seen the "beast", as she called it. Pete, Robbie figured, joined up because he just wanted friends who accepted him, and couldn't care less about what they were all up to so long as he was with them. As for himself, Robbie had seen tracks in the woods that countless trips to the library and an equal number of internet searches couldn't identify. Regardless, that was what they did together, hunt the monster in the woods.

They geared up, shrugging on pre-loaded backpacks, handing out radios, and then left the basement and their bikes behind. Megan took the lead as the group headed out along the well-worn trail they used to get up into the woods behind the farmhouse.

****

The smell of formaldehyde was worse than the crap he'd smelt in the woods, Bernard thought, as he stood in the autopsy room where Waller was at work on the first of the bodies. Deputy Miller had come with him as he'd left Clarkson in charge of the crime scene up in the woods. And besides, Miller was the best and brightest officer working for him. Bernard wanted her take on things. Maybe she could make sense of the crap he was dealing with. He sure as hell couldn't. The slaughter of four men, two of them armed, and the freaky tracks around where they were attacked. . .Bernard sighed and shook his head.

"Coffee, Sheriff?" Miller asked, offering him a cup she'd just got from Waller's office.

"Thanks," Bernard managed a weak smile for her, taking the cup, and downing a hot, black swig from it.

"Whelp, Sheriff," Waller stopped his examination of the body on the table and looked up at him and Miller. "The good news is that you for sure got some kind of animal attack here. These wounds were made by something's teeth and claws."

"So what's the bad news?" Miller asked Waller before Bernard could.

Sliding off his blood covered gloves, Waller answered, "I can't even guess at what kind of animal."

"What's that supposed to mean?" Bernard pressed Waller.

"Exactly what it sounds like," Waller said. "I ain't never, and I mean never, even heard of an animal that could make these type of wounds, Sheriff. The amount of strength it would have to have. . . it'd be as much or more than the largest bears around these parts but the claw marks, their spread and shape, couldn't have possibly come from a bear."

"Why not?" Miller frowned.

"Too far apart," Waller explained. "Their positioning is much more akin to that of say what your fingernails would make if your hand were several times larger."

"Are you suggesting a primate killed that man?" Miller eyed Waller.

Bernard had taken another swig of coffee and nearly spat it out before he could swallow it.

"Waller," Bernard's voice was loud and deep. "This is North Carolina. There aren't any primates around here."

The coroner shrugged. "Deputy Miller is right. A primate would be my best guess too. I know how crazy that sounds, Sheriff, I do, but those wounds. . ."

"And how exactly would a primate make its

way here?" Bernard challenged Waller. "Could it even survive in these parts?"

"Just calling things as I see them, Sheriff," Waller shrugged again.

Sheriff Bernard and Deputy Miller left Waller alone to examine the other bodies that had been brought in.

The day outside was a hot one without a cloud in the sky. Bernard blinked as the harsh rays of the midday sun struck his eyes. Miller had ridden with him in his patrol car. As they approached the vehicle, Miller asked, "You want me to drive, Sheriff?"

The glance he sent her way gave Miller her answer. She headed for the passenger side and got in as Bernard slid into the driver's seat. Bernard slammed his door. He'd hoped that Waller would bring some sanity back into this investigation not add to its insanity. His fingers gripped the key he'd just shoved in the patrol car's ignition but didn't crank up the patrol car. Bernard looked over at Miller and sucked in a deep breath.

"Did you get to see the prints that were found?" he asked her.

Miller shook her head.

Bernard took out his phone. Clarkson had sent him shots of the tracks so he'd have them if needed. He hadn't felt like there was any point even mentioning the photos to Waller. The coroner wasn't an outdoor kind of guy and tracks were outside of the man's wheelhouse anyway. He called up the clearest of the shots and handed his phone to Miller.

"Holy crap," Miller muttered. "Are those for real?"

"As far as we can tell," Bernard nodded. "There's nothing to suggest that they aren't."

"We're totally screwed on this one huh, bossman?" Miller frowned. "If the press gets word of those tracks, we're gonna have one hell of a panic, not to mention God only knows how many people heading up there to look for Bigfoot."

"Bigfoot," Bernard repeated the word with utter contempt and disgust. "Damn it, Miller. I've been in law enforcement for a long time and I've seen some strange crap in my days but nothing ever like this. Monsters aren't supposed to be real."

"It's sure looking like this one is," she told him.

"And if it is, what in the hell are we supposed to do about it?" Bernard asked.

"Our jobs," Miller's voice was flat. "We're just gonna need to quiet on the details as we do them."

Bernard nodded. "I think Clarkson's already got the keep it quiet part covered, at least with the paramedics who were at the scene, and

Waller isn't going to talk. That's just not who he is. There is one person I think we need to pay a visit to though."

Miller cocked an eyebrow at him.

"Paul was at the scene this morning. We had to escort him down the mountain," Bernard said through gritted teeth.

Her eyes went wide at his revelation. "That's some fragging bad luck right there. The one time that A hole stumbles onto a real story, it had to be this one. You sure paying him a visit's going to be enough to stop him from writing everything up?"

"We're gonna make damn sure it is," Bernard promised, throwing the patrol car into reverse, and nearly flooring the gas. Its wheel spun out some as he whipped the car around and left the parking lot. Bernard didn't turn on the siren though. He figured they'd draw enough attention as it was.

****

"Hold up," Megan ordered, raising a hand indicating for the others behind her to stop. She'd heard something strange up ahead of them.

"What is it?" Warren blurted out.

"Sssshh," Brently nudged him.

"Don't you shush me, chubby," Warren hammered a fist into Brently's shoulder.

"Ow!" Brently cried out.

"Shut up!" Pete shouted. "Both of you!"

Robbie was shaking his head. He moved to stand beside Megan.

"I thought I heard something," Megan explained.

"It's the woods. Things make noise out here. Just listen to them," Robbie gestured with his thumbs towards the other guys.

Megan met his eyes with hers and Robbie could see that the joke he'd just made was a mistake.

"I'm serious," Megan's voice was low and cold.

Robbie swallowed, trying to think of what to say next but before he could open his mouth again something came rushing through the trees towards them.

"Look out!" Megan yelled, shoving Robbie off his feet. He toppled over, landing hard on his butt in the grass. Megan dived back in the other direction as a deer bounded, at a break neck pace, between where they had been standing.

"Holy!" Pete yelped as he and the rest of group scattered, getting out of the freaked out animal's path.

Then the deer was gone as quickly as it had come.

"What the hell!" Warren roared, looking in the direction the deer had fled in.

Robbie hopped up from the ground, hands

dusting dirt and leaves from the back of his pants.

"Something must have spooked the hell out of that poor deer," Megan said to no one in particular. "It didn't even care that we were here."

"That was seriously messed up," Brently commented.

"From the look on your face, I thought you were going to pee your pants, man," Warren badgered him.

"Ease up right now," Pete warned, taking a step closer to Warren. "I ain't kidding."

Warren raised his hands, palms out, in a gesture of surrender.

"Okay, man. Okay," Warren said.

"Uh, guys," Brently spoke up. "That deer was scared out of its mind. Don't you think we should be getting out of here too before we find out what it was running from?"

"You don't think. . ." Robbie started.

"I do," Megan nodded. "Today could be the day we finally find the monster up here."

They all exchanged half excited, half worried glances with each other. Robbie, for his part, hadn't really expected that day to ever come. He didn't know about the others.

Brently had taken out his phone to use as a camera. His goal, like Megan's, was to get proof that the thing existed, though his reasons were different. Brently sought to discover a new species and get his name in the science journals and history books. Megan just wanted to prove that she wasn't crazy like lots of the kids at school still believed she was from her younger days. Back then, Megan told everyone who would listen about seeing the monster outside her house the night of her tenth birthday. Robbie didn't know if Megan regretted doing that now or not because of her passionate belief in the truth though he did wonder if it had happened now instead of back then, if Megan would be quieter about it without proof. But then, that was why she was up here, to find proof of the monster she desperately wanted.

Seeing the phone clutched so tightly in Brently's hand made Robbie realize something else. If the monster were up here and real, they were ill equipped to do anything but snap photos and make a run for it.

"Quiet!" Megan barked in a harsh whisper just barely loud enough to be heard.

Something was rushing through the woods towards them but not from the direction the deer had come. It was coming at their right flank. Robbie wanted to shout out for everyone to run but didn't.

Warren jerked a small revolver out from the back of his pants and took aim at the noise.

Megan's eyes went wide as she saw the

weapon. Robbie figured his did too. He recognized the weapon as a Smith and Wesson Bodyguard .38. Warren had likely lifted it off his mother. Robbie knew that she worked at Bogart's, the town's most popular place to eat, and often had to make her way home alone, late at night. He should have known that Warren would have always been carrying a weapon with him every time they came up here to look for the monster. Unlike Megan and Brently, Warren didn't want proof that the beast was real. He wanted vengeance for it killing his father, whether or not the thing really had.

The pistol cracked as Warren squeezed its trigger. The .38 bucked in his hands as it spat a bullet which streaked into the trees, slamming into a low hanging branch next to the head of the man who came bursting onto the trail at them. The man dropped into a firing position, like the professional he was, his own gun aimed at Warren.

"Drop the damn gun right now, kid, or I'll drop you!" the man yelled.

Pete reached out to slap Warren's .38 from his hands before Warren could even move. Robbie thanked God for that as it sunk in that the man was wearing a deputy's uniform.

"Deputy Clarkson!" Megan cried out.

Clarkson wasn't listening to her, though. He rushed forward again, grabbing up Warren's revolver from where it lay in the grass while keeping his pistol aimed at him.

"You kids better have one hell of an explanation for what just happened," Clarkson snapped.

"I'm sorry!" Warren blurted out.

"We're all sorry," Megan added. "We thought you were. . ."

"You thought I was what?" Deputy Clarkson demanded.

"Sir," Robbie said, drawing Clarkson's attention to him. "A deer just charged through here in a panic, scared the crap out of us. We thought there had to be something pretty nasty chasing it and that you were it."

Robbie saw Deputy Clarkson look them all over.

"I don't give a crap," Clarkson growled. "You just took a shot at me. Do you even have any idea how much trouble you're in?"

"We didn't know it was you, sir!" Pete protested on Warren's behalf.

"Yeah and that's the only thing that's keeping me from throwing the book at you, kid," Clarkson still had his gun in his hand, ready to swing it up if need be. "What the hell are you even doing up here anyway?"

None of them answered.

Clarkson spat. "I guess you kids missed the news that this whole area up here is off limits."

"Off limits?" Megan frowned.

"You heard me," Deputy Clarkson said. "I want all of you to head back the way you came right now and stay the hell out of these parts. You got me?"

"Yes sir," Robbie said. "We'll go right now."

"Wait," Warren spoke up. "What about my gun?"

Deputy Clarkson snorted with a sneer on his face. "Mr. Huffman, you'd better just be dang glad I am letting you go at all for now and I promise you, you and your mother will be seeing me later on."

Robbie saw Warren's hand coming up, likely to flip Clarkson off. Catching his arm and holding it, Robbie kept him from getting in even more trouble than he already was.

"Let's go," Pete said, motioning for the others to follow him. Roughly shoving him around, Robbie made sure that Warren did.

****

The clearing where the rough gravel road ended was massive. There was room for all three of their trucks. Of course, Howard and his crew were partly responsible for that. When they'd arrived, expanding the clearing was their first day of work. It had been hard going but for the amount they were being paid, no one on his crew was complaining. The town of Canton had given them a contract to clear the way for a road through the woods up here from Haywood County to Buncombe County. Both counties, long term, wanted to develop the land up here but for right now, a road to do that on was where they were starting. Howard didn't really care. All that mattered to him was the work. His business was on the edge of needing to downsize before the contract had come along. The contract would not only prevent that but also give Howard a chance to figure out the future.

Today was Saturday so the bulk of his people were off. Howard had only been able to con Smith and Pressley into working overtime. He could hear the roar of their chainsaws in the distance. It was a strangely comforting sound. Howard smiled, leaning against the closest of the three big, yellow logging trucks. Whipping a cigarette out of his pocket, Howard lit it up, taking a deep drag. He exhaled the smoke slowly, savoring the taste of it, something that wasn't an option at home anymore. His wife, Brenda, had told him that if he didn't quit, she wouldn't be sticking around much longer. It pissed Howard off but the two of them were high school sweethearts with a decade of marriage already behind them. Sure, their relationship wasn't perfect. Whose was? But it was worth saving if he could. Besides, with his job, all he had to do was give up something at home and

Brenda would never know the difference. Out here no one but his crew were going to know and none of them would be telling her about it. They all knew damn well what would happen to them if they did.

Howard opened the door of the main truck and reached in to get his cell phone from where he'd left it on the driver's seat. Swiping its screen, he tried to get online and cursed. The signal up here was spotty as hell even with the mobile hotspot he'd brought with him. It was the damnedest thing. Howard couldn't explain it. He wasn't a tech head like most kids were these days.

There was a sudden shift in the noise coming from the trees along the path where Smith and Pressley were working. It took Howard a second to realize what it was. One of the chainsaws had stopped. What the hell? he wondered. It wasn't break time.

A grumpy scowl on his face, Howard tossed his cigarette down and ground it out with the sole of his boot. He started walking towards the edge of the clearing, ready to tear whichever of his guys it was slacking a new one. The other chainsaw fell silent like the first as one of the guys started screaming. Howard flinched at the sound of sheer terror in the voice. An accident was just about the worst thing that could happen to his business right now. His legs pumped beneath him as Howard broke into a sprint, running in the direction of the screams. He hadn't even reached the edge of the clearing when Smith burst out from the trees ahead of him. Howard could see red on Smith's clothes and swallowed hard. They were screwed if whatever happened was anywhere near as bad as he was imagining. Then he realized that though he was in plain view, Smith wasn't stopping or even slowing down to get his help.

"Run!" Smith cried out at him. "That thing is right behind me!"

Howard didn't have a clue what the hell Smith was talking about.

"It killed Pressley!" Smith was heading straight for the closest of their trucks and from the way he was bucking it, Howard could tell the man was determined to get the hell out of there as fast as he could. He made a grab for Smith as the man ran by him but missed, his hand groping empty air.

Having failed to stop Smith, Howard hesitated, trying to decide whether to go after him or run on into the woods to check on Pressley. He was still standing there as the creature tore its way out of the woods in front of him. Howard's eyes went wide and his bladder let loose, hot liquid flowing down his thighs and legs, soaking the front of his pants. The thing that was coming at him stood at least eight feet tall. Its eyes were so intensely yellow, it was like they were glowing. Thick brown hair covered the creature's body from head to toe and huge muscles rippled as it ran on two legs like a man. The claws of its far too human-like hands gleamed in the sunlight, wet with blood.

Howard started to turn and run after Smith but the creature was so fast, it had already reached him. A hair-covered hand struck Howard, knocking him out of the creature's path and sending him flying through the air like a toy that a child had tossed aside in anger. He hit the ground, rolling and bouncing across the clearing. Sharp pain erupted from his shoulder and Howard knew it was hurt bad. His head jerked up and around in the creature's wake as he watched the thing closing on Smith, who had managed to reach the closest truck and get its door open. Smith whirled about at the sound of the thing's snarling approach just in time to have one of its clawed hands plunge into his abdomen, angling upwards beneath his ribcage. When the creature yanked the hand back out of Smith it was clutching long strands of purple, red slicked entrails. Smith was howling like a dying cat right up until the creature's other hand came down atop his head. His skull was crunched inward with such force that Smith's eyes burst out of their sockets. Smith's corpse crumpled onto the gravel of the clearing at the creature's feet while Howard leapt back onto his.

The creature was between him and the trucks so Howard ran into the woods. There was no other option. Having seen how fast the thing was, Howard figured he was as good as dead. The creature would overtake him before he could get very far and he knew it. Pushing his body to its limits and pouring on all the speed he could muster, he dodged low lying limbs and jumped over patches of thick roots that grew up through the ground. Then Howard spotted the chainsaw lying not more than a few yards ahead of him. Smith must have dropped it there as he'd made his run for the clearing. Howard altered his course, going straight for the chainsaw. It wasn't much of a weapon but it was a damn sight better than facing the thing chasing after him empty handed.

"Frag me," Howard grunted as his hands closed on the chainsaw and he picked it up. The thing was heavy as hell, twenty pounds or more. Bracing its main body on one leg, Howard yanked the chainsaw's starter row like a madman, pulling it over and over until he was rewarded with a fierce roar. The chainsaw was unwieldy and difficult to get into a good fighting position. Howard readied it as best he could, turning to see the creature bounding through the woods, already only yards from where he stood. He revved the chainsaw, hoping to scare the hulking creature enough to drive it away. No such luck.

Howard thrust the chainsaw forward at the creature's chest as it charged him. He got lucky and the blade cut into the meat there at just the right angle to slide into it easily. The creature shrieked in pain and anger as Howard shoved the chainsaw's blade deeper into its body. Blood and small chunks of meat flew all over him, splattering onto his cheeks, arms, and hands. The thing's blood was hot and sticky. Howard lost his hold on the chainsaw as the beast lurched away from him. The chainsaw stopped running but was still imbedded in the creature's chest. Rivers of blood ran out from the wound, drenching its brown hair, turning it red. The beast gave a final pained grunt and tumbled over, collapsing into the grass. It wasn't dead, just hurt. The creature's overly large hands took hold of the chainsaw's body and slowly pulled its blade out. Blood spurted from the wound as the blade popped loose. Not wanting to allow the creature to get up, Howard's eyes flicked about the area around him, searching for something, anything else he could use as a weapon. There was a large piece of wood that was close enough for him to get his hands on. Howard ran to where the creature was rolling over onto its side, blood continuing to pour from its chest. Hefting the wood like a baseball bat, he brought it down with both hands on the side of the creature's face with a jarring thud. The impact knocked the creature back onto the ground. Howard raised the wood above his head again, swinging it downward a second time. The wood smashed the creature's right eye socket with a sickening crunching noise. Partially blind, the creature snarled, lashing out at his legs. Howard tried to jump out of its reach but wasn't able to. A large hand locked onto his left shin. Its claws sunk into his flesh as Howard screamed and his leg was yanked from under him. He went down, a mass of flailing limbs, his makeshift weapon flying out of his hands. Landing flat on his back, the breath was knocked from his lungs, leaving Howard gasping for air.

Kicking out with his other leg, Howard slammed a booted foot into the creature's face aiming for its already fractured eye socket. The blow made contact with another sick crunch of bone that caused the creature to loose a thunderous howl. Releasing the hold on his leg and heaving itself up, the creature stood towering over Howard. It was his turn to roll as he avoided the oversized fist that plummeted downward at his head. The fist slammed into the dirt where his head had been only a fraction of a second before as Howard scrambled to get away from the creature. Making it to his feet, Howard ran like hell without looking back. He heard the creature roar behind him and kept running. It was all he could do, no matter how futile it might be. Heavy footfalls drew ever closer behind him. The weird thing was they seemed to be coming from his left flank. Howard zagged to the right, cutting sharply around the thick trunk of a larger tree and thudded straight into the body of something huge and covered in hair. Howard felt the thing's arms close around him. As they tightened and his ribs broke beneath his flesh, his head lolling sideways, he saw the creature that had been chasing come to a stop, watching him be crushed. As his mouth filled with his own blood from the internal injury being inflicted upon him, Howard gave up the fight.

****

Paul was sitting at his desk as Sheriff Bernard came bursting in, slamming the door inward so hard that its knob was driven into the wood of the interior wall of the office where it made contact. Deputy Miller was with him. Paul leaped up from his seat, indignant, and startled by his sudden entrance.

"Sheriff Bernard!" Paul blurted out. "What is the meaning of this?"

Bernard shoved the reporter roughly back into the seat he'd been in.

Paul looked up at him with fear in his eyes.

"We're going to have a little talk now, Paul,

about what you saw this morning," Bernard snarled.

"You can't treat me like this, Sheriff," Paul said firmly though he was trembling in his chair. "I have rights."

"I haven't even threatened you yet, Paul," Bernard said, leaning over the reporter's desk with one hand on its top supporting his weight.

"No," Paul frowned. "But that's what's coming next, isn't it?"

"Look," Miller cut in, "You weren't supposed to be in those woods this morning and you know it, Paul. What you saw up there. . ."

"What I saw up there scared the crap out of me," Paul admitted. "The town has a right to know what you people are dealing with up there."

"I don't know what I am dealing with yet," Bernard said. "How the hell can you pretend to?"

"Sheriff, Deputy Miller, I know what I saw," Paul told them. "Whatever killed those guys couldn't have been human. I think we can all agree on that."

"We don't know that for sure," Miller argued. "We're still going over all the evidence."

Paul laughed. "Yeah, right."

"And you writing up some story about something in the woods that's killing people, what's that going to do, Paul? Rile folks up?

Start a panic? Maybe even send a bunch of good ole boys with rifles and shotguns up there where they're just as likely to shoot each other as be of any help?" Bernard raged.

"My job is to report the things that matter in this town, Sheriff," Paul countered. "How people respond to it isn't on me."

"Oh but it is," Miller said, shaking her head.

"You can't stop me, Sheriff," Paul leaned back in his seat, calmer than he'd been than when they first burst in.

"No, Paul, I guess I can't," Sheriff Bernard scowled. "But I can ask you not to."

"He wasn't exaggerating, Paul. Things are bad and you writing about them right now will only make things worse, not better," Miller pleaded. "We're not asking you to not do your job. We're just asking for some time to get a handle on things before you do."

Bernard was impressed by Miller's fluid switch of tactics in dealing with Paul. It was as if she somehow sensed what would work with him where his own attempt at intimidation had failed.

"Okay," Paul nodded. "I can give you a day. How's that?"

"You could give us more if you wanted," Bernard pointed out.

"A day," Paul said. "Take it or leave it."

"We'll take it," Miller smiled. "Thank you,

Paul."

Bernard and Miller left his office. After they were in the patrol car, Bernard asked, "That went a lot better than I thought it would but do you think we can really trust him?"

Miller nodded. "I think so."

Bernard cranked the car, glancing over at her before throwing it in reverse to back out of the parking space in front of the newspaper's main door. "I hope you're right."

****

The patrol car came to a stop in the clearing near the trio of bright yellow trucks of the company the town had hired to clear out a way over the mountain into Buncombe County. Deputy Russell was in the driver's seat. Deputy Gillan had ridden up with him.

"Clarkson always give us the crap jobs," Russell complained, thumping the dashboard in frustration. "That bastard could have come up here himself, ya know?"

Gillan shrugged. "Could be worse."

Russell scowled at her. Gillan was half his age, smarter than he was, and far more attractive with her red hair and pale skin. He couldn't stand her most days. Back when he'd started with the department, women deputies were almost unheard of, now they were everywhere. The world was changing, and in his opinion, not for the better.

"Let's just get this over with already," Russell huffed.

Clarkson had sent them to order the work crew out of the woods for the time being. The sheriff's declaration that the woods were off limits apparently included these folks too. Russell knew they weren't going to be happy about it either. Crews like this worked on a timetable and being forced to take a day or maybe even days off would sure as hell screw it up.

"Hold up," Gillan said, stopping Russell as he started to get out of the patrol car.

"What?" Russell snapped at her.

"Take a look around, Russell," she told him. "There's no one here."

"So?" Russell said. "They're just on up in the woods working."

"I don't think so," Gillan shook her head. "You hear any chainsaws or other equipment?"

Russell listened for a second. Damn her, Gillan was right. He couldn't hear anything outside of the car. It was like the entire woods around them were silent. There weren't even birds chirping.

"Well that's pretty damn creepy," Russell commented.

"What are you thinking?" Gillan asked.

"That we should just call this crew in as

missing and head back to town," Russell admitted.

"You know we can't," Gillan gave him a sharp glare.

Russell sighed, knowing she was right.

Gillan drew her Glock 22. "Come on. Let's go find these guys and get out of here."

Russell, grunting his agreement, got out with her. They both stood next to their own sides of the patrol car for a moment, scanning the area around them intently.

"Damn!" Gillan shouted suddenly and ran towards one the trucks. Russell didn't have a clue what she had seen that he hadn't but knew it couldn't be anything good. Then he saw it too. There was blood splattered on the hood of the truck and its driver's side door. It was dried and partially masked by how the shadows of the trees around the clearing fell over the vehicle.

"Someone was killed here," Gillan told him and he knew she was right.

She pointed at the ground and slowly raised her finger towards the trees. "Whatever killed them dragged the body that way afterwards."

Russell spat into the grass as the muscles of his stomach tightened. This was some royally F.U.B.A.R.-ed crap they were dealing with. If the guys of this crew were all dead too, that would mean seven lives would have been lost since last night up here in these woods. The sheriff had ordered that no one talk about what was going on because he didn't want to start a panic in town. Russell was beginning to understand why.

"We'll go check it out," Russell nodded, "but first. . ."

He walked back to the patrol car, popping the trunk. Russell noticed that Gillan didn't make any move to stop him as he got out the shotgun from it. Working its pump, Russell chambered a round. His expression was grim as he turned to Gillan.

"You ready now?" Gillan quipped.

"Hell no," Russell shook his head, "but like you said, it's our job, ain't it?"

Gillan nodded. "I'll take point. You cover me if anything comes our way."

Both of them had seen the crime scene of the murder that had happened last night, how those guys had been torn apart, some even gnawed on. Gillan had told him that even Sheriff Bernard was spooked by it all. Bernard was tough as nails. That fragger wasn't someone you wanted to screw with. . .ever. If he was really worried, the whole freaking town should be, including them. There were whispers that whatever killed those guys wasn't human or any sort of animal that a sane person could believe existed. Russell hoped that's all they were too. . . just whispers. . . rumors born of nerves and a lack of answers.

Walking at a cautious pace, Gillan followed the trail of blood in the grass. It led into the woods. The sun was bright in the sky above and the day was hotter than it had any right to be. Russell was sweating but not from the heat. There usually wasn't much trouble in town, not much more than bar fights and teenage rowdiness. This crap they were dealing with now. . . Russell would never admit it but he was freaked out as crap. He was glad Gillan was in the lead. The lady had balls. He'd give her that. His knuckles were white from the pressure of his grip on the shotgun he carried.

Gillan came to an abrupt halt ahead of him.

"You smell that?" she asked.

He did. The stench was horrid. It made him want to hurl but Russell fought away the sickness. He didn't have time for that. The smell was like rotting meat, cooking slowly in the hot rays of the sun, combined with an odor of vomit. But there was something else too. Something he couldn't quite place. Sort of like some kind of heavy musk, filthy, like that of a skunk.

"Maybe we should go call this in and wait for backup," Russell suggested.

Gillan wasn't having that. She frowned at him and got moving again, holding her Glock at the ready in a two-handed grip.

"Come on," Gillan ordered.

She didn't outrank him. The way she'd just

bossed him around ticked Russell off. Very uncharacteristically, he let it slide. There were larger things to deal with at the moment. If they didn't have each others' backs, there sure as hell wasn't anyone else out here to look to for help.

"Russell!" Gillan cried out and he saw why. Ahead of them in the grass was a corpse. Well, pieces of a corpse at any rate.

"Damn. . ." Russell muttered.

A man's leg, mostly stripped of flesh, lay next to a matching arm. Something had been eating on both of them. The guy's head was there too, broken, and leaking congealed brain matter. The eye sockets of the head were empty as if something had scooped them out.

Gillan lost it, doubling over and throwing up her breakfast onto the ground. Her body heaved as the vomit splattered all over her shoes. Russell watched her, not having a clue how to help, until she was done. Gillan righted herself, wiping at her lips with the backside of her left hand.

"Sorry," she said weakly, looking embarrassed and ashamed.

"Screw this," Russell grumbled. "We shouldn't be out here on our own and you know it, Gillan. What if the thing that did this is still hanging around?"

"You noticed the tracks too, huh?" Gillan commented.

Russell looked down and saw them. There were strange, huge tracks all over the place. They looked like something that might belong to a barefoot giant. Before he could respond about them though a low moan arose from nearby in the trees. Russell didn't know why but it made him shudder.

"Aw jeez. . ." Gillan said. "What the crap is that?"

"I don't care, Gillan," Russell glared at her. "It's time for us to go."

She shook her head. "It could be someone that survived."

And with that, Gillan was bounding away towards the noise. Russell held his ground for a second before finally cursing and then hurrying after the redhead.

Gillan screamed as he burst into the small clearing between the trees after her. His eyes went straight to the thing lying there. It wasn't a man. That much was for sure. But it was humanoid. Lots of its body was shaped like that of a man's. Russell jerked up his shotgun, bracing it against his shoulder, aiming it at the thing in front of them even though from the looks of it, the creature wouldn't be getting up anytime soon. It was drenched in blood. The thing's chest had been savaged and was ripped open to the point that he could see the white bone of its ribs. One of its eyes was gone too. The socket the eye had been in was a smashed in mess of gore.

The creature moaned louder at the sight of them, raising one of its arms in their direction. That was enough to trigger an instinctive reaction from Russell. He squeezed the trigger of his shotgun. It thundered, the sound of its blast echoing in the trees, and spat a heavy slug that punched a wide hole in the creature's forehead. The thing's extended arm collapsed limply, thudding onto the ground next to its body.

"How. . . How fragging big is that thing?" Gillan stammered.

"Can't say for sure," Russell answered, chambering another round, "Maybe eight, nine feet if it were standing up, I'd guess. I think the better question though is what the hell is it?"

Gillan stared at him as if were an idiot. "You're joking, right? That thing is a Sasquatch. It has to be."

Russell wasn't able to argue with her. He'd definitely never seen anything like the creature before and it did look enough like the Sasquatch you saw in horror films or on TV to sure pass for one. It was the main source of the musky, rot-like stench too. Being this close to the thing was almost unbearable for him. Lowering his shotgun since there was no longer any question about whether the thing was dead or not, he'd made sure of that, Russell took a couple of steps back, covering his mouth and nose with one hand.

"What happened to its chest?" Russell said through his hand. "Looks like someone cut it up with a freaking chainsaw."

"That's likely exactly what went down," Gillan nodded. "This work crew would have been carrying chainsaws and using them. Guess one of them got lucky."

"Not lucky enough," Russell huffed. "I'm betting we won't find any survivors here."

There was dark red smeared in the hair around the sasquatch's mouth suggesting that despite being mortally wounded, the thing had managed to have its dinner before bleeding out.

"Yeah," Gillan agreed. "I hate to say it but I think you're right. If anyone was still alive here, that shotgun blast would have caused them to come running to us."

"You know we're gonna be famous, right?" Russell chuckled. All the tension and fear he'd been feeling died with the beast he had shot, draining out of him. "We're not just the first people to find proof that Bigfoot is real but we're the first people to kill one, too."

"Is that really what you're thinking about right now?" Gillan scowled.

"Can you blame me?" Russell smirked.

"Forget about that crap," Gillan barked.

"There are two more people out here we need to find."

"You mean two more bodies," Russell corrected her.

"Come on," Gillan said.

"Whoa! Hold up," Russell stopped her. "We can't just leave this thing lying here. It's too valuable. And before you even say anything about that, you know Bernard's gonna wanna know it's here as soon as possible."

"Fine," Gillan sighed. "I'll stay. You head to the car and let the sheriff know."

"Why is it you're the one that's staying?" Russell challenged her.

"What? You don't trust me?" Gillan was flaming mad now. Russell could see that last bit had pushed her too far.

"Screw you, Russell," she spat and stormed off into the trees, leaving him standing alone with the dead creature.

Russell shrugged. If Gillan wanted to be ticked at him, that was her choice. It wasn't going to matter soon anyway. Once word got out about the beast and that they'd been the ones to bring it down, the TV offers, book offers, and cash, would start pouring in. Russell figured he wasn't going to be stuck working as a deputy in a small town like Canton for very much longer. For the first time in a very, very long time, he'd caught a break and planned to make the most of it.

His attention returned to the dead creature as Russell waited on Gillan to come back. From the thickness of the muscles on the thing's arms, it had to have been strong as hell. Russell whistled at the sight of them. Damn, he thought, if they'd wandered on this thing and it hadn't been almost dead already, it would've likely been them that was worm food now, not it.

Glancing at his watch, Russell began to wonder what was taking Gillan so long. He wondered if she was complaining to Bernard about him. So what if she was, right? he thought. It really didn't matter anymore. Killing the Bigfoot made him a fragging hero! The witch could say whatever she wanted about him to the sheriff.

Russell heard a series of sharp cracks from the direction of the main clearing where their patrol car was. There was no mistaking what they were, shots being fired, in rapid succession, by a Glock 22.

"Fragging A!" Russell shouted, knowing that Gillan was in trouble. He didn't want to leave the Bigfoot body but couldn't stand by and not go to her. He punched the closest tree trunk in anger and frustration. The bark tore up the skin of his knuckles. It hurt like hell but the pain helped Russell focus on what he needed to do. Running through the trees, he sprinted for the clearing where the work trucks and their patrol car were parked.

Bursting out of the woods, shotgun at the ready, Russell had no idea what to expect. With the beast dead there shouldn't be anything else out here to threaten them. He saw the patrol car. Its driver's side door was . . . just gone. Something had torn it from the car. There was blood dripping out of the car and he saw Gillan. Russell knew at once she was dead from the posture of her body. It was bent over, head face down against the car's dashboard.

Russell slowed his run, coming to a stop a few feet away from the patrol car. His eyes darted about in an attempt to locate whoever the hell it was that had killed Gillan. Had one of the workers come back out of the woods so messed up from his encounter with the Bigfoot that he'd killed Gillan? That didn't make much sense but sadly it was the best explanation Russell was able to come up with on the fly.

There wasn't anyone around that he could see. That didn't mean a lot. There were plenty of places to hide that would put them out of his line of sight. Russell continued to look around from where he was standing until he happened to glance at the ground and saw them. There were tracks from something heavy enough to have left them in the harder earth of the clearing that led up to the patrol car. Russell swallowed hard.

He'd seen those type of tracks before. They were Bigfoot tracks. His insides went cold. Neither he or Gillan had even thought of it. At least if she had, she hadn't mentioned it. More than one of the beasts being up here sure as hell didn't seem possible. But what if there was more than one Bigfoot in these woods?

Carefully, slowly, Russell crept towards the patrol car, knowing that he couldn't help Gillan. Nonetheless, he needed to get to the radio. Sure, he had a cell in his pocket but up here, on the mountain, it wasn't more than a plastic paperweight. That radio was his lifeline.

Something roared, deep in the woods, to the west. Russell spun in that direction, his shotgun braced against his shoulder in a firing position. He nearly wet his pants as another roar came from somewhere a hell of a lot closer to the east of the clearing. There was more than one Bigfoot up here! God only knew how many there were. A family? A tribe? A freaking war party?

Russell rushed to the patrol car and grabbed Gillan's body by her shoulder, flinging her out of the car onto the ground. Her corpse landed on its back, wide open, dead eyes staring up into the midday sun. The entire lower half of her face was little more than jagged bits of fractured bone and pulped flesh. The car's steering wheel was broken exactly where Gillan's face would have struck it if she had been sitting in the driver's seat and something smashed it forward. The dash was dented and cracked too, slicked by Gillan's blood. He might not have liked Gillan but that didn't mean he'd wanted her dead and sure as hell not like this. His heart sank as Russell noticed that she was clutching the car's radio in her right hand. She must have been holding it when the thing attacked her. Her Glock 22 was clutched in her other hand.

A loud growl drew Russell's attention. He looked around to see a nine foot tall Sasquatch standing only a few yards away. The creature hadn't made a sound as it closed on him. Russell's mind reeled at that fact. Something so large and bulky. . .

The Sasquatch's growl became a snarl as it charged forward. Russell's shotgun boomed as he squeezed its trigger. The weapon's blast hit the beast, nearly point blank, dead center in its chest. It didn't stop the monster though. The Sasquatch batted Russell's shotgun out of his hands, and slammed him into the side of the patrol car just behind the driver's seat. Russell squirmed and wriggled, trying to escape its hold as the thing's clawed fingers twisted about inside the flesh of his arms. In desperation, Russell jerked up his knee between the Sasquatch's legs. It thudded home there. The Sasquatch squealed and released him. Russell flopped onto the ground at its feet. He started crawling towards the trunk of the car but the beast recovered so quickly Russell didn't make it more than a couple of feet. The creature reached out, grabbing him up as if Russell didn't weigh anything, and slammed him into the side of the car so hard the metal there dented inward as he struck it. One blow wasn't enough for the beast though. It continued to smash Russell into the car several more times before finally letting go and dropping his broken and bashed up corpse.

The clearing was quiet again as the Sasquatch knelt next to Russell's body. The beast ripped a handful of flesh loose from it and then began to eat.

****

"That was crap!" Warren yelled. He was still fuming about Deputy Clarkson taking his gun.

"Dude," Pete sighed, "Let it go."

"Yeah," Megan agreed, "It could have gone a lot worse, Warren. You could be in jail right now, ya know?"

Brently and Robbie were following along behind the three of them. Robbie heard what Megan said and wondered just how in the heck Warren had avoided jail. He supposed it wasn't out of the question yet as Deputy Clarkson had told them he would be meeting up with Warren and his mother later but. . . something was off about the whole mess. Deputy Clarkson should really have taken Warren in right then and there. A teenager with a gun who'd almost shot him? Oh yeah, that should have been a bigger deal even in a small town like Canton. . . which left Robbie believing that something a lot worse was going on in the woods. Clarkson had told them that the sheriff had put the woods off limits to the general public. That didn't make any freaking sense either. Robbie knew the sheriff couldn't really block it all off. It just wasn't possible without calling in the national guard or something.

"Thank God!" Pete exclaimed as the edge of the woods opened up onto the road outside of Ammon's Diner. They had headed here rather than back to their "base of operations" because Megan was hungry and she'd been in the lead. Most of the time, no one in the group argued with her. Part of it was because she was a really attractive girl who actually wanted to spend time with them but it was also because they'd all found out the hard way just how rough Megan could get when she was mad.

"Food!" Brently shouted, darting after Megan and Pete as they burst out from the trees and ran across the road into the diner's parking lot.

Warren didn't run after them so Robbie caught up to him, the two of them walking side by side.

"You really did get lucky, Warren," he said.

Warren shot him an angry glare but otherwise didn't respond.

One would think that a small town like Canton would have quite a few "mom and pop" style places to eat but it didn't. Ammon's was the only place in town. All the other places were just the same chain restaurants that you'd find anywhere else throughout the country. That wasn't the only thing that made Ammon's special though. The diner was hella old, having been around for nearly fifty years. It wasn't the social mecca of the town like in days gone by but was still the place to eat if you wanted good, freshly cooked food.

The parking lot was mostly empty, the dinner crowd having mostly departed already. In another twenty minutes or so, it would be full out dark. Robbie was glad to be in town again and grateful for the streetlights that were beginning to spring to life up and down the road. The ones in the parking lot were already on.

A small bell jingled loudly as the group of teenagers entered. Megan, Brently, and Pete hurried to take seats in the group's usual booth near the diner's rear. Robbie saw Warren take a look around, clearly seeing if his mother was still working or not. There was no sign of her. Warren seemed to relax a bit and turned to him.

"I gotta hit the bathroom, man," Warren said. "Let them know where I'm at."

"Sure," Robbie grinned. "I can do that."

"Hey! Come on!" Brently was waving him on over to their booth.

Robbie slid into it, taking a seat next to Pete. Brently and Megan were sitting across from them. Megan held a menu in her hands, scanning it, though he was sure that she must have every item on it memorized by now.

Taking his own look around, Robbie noticed aside from Mr. and Mrs. Ammon themselves, the only other people in the diner were a stranger, he guessed to be a truck driver that was passing through who sat at the main window and Ms. Beasley, who sat alone at the diner's counter. She looked just as sad and haunted as ever. Robbie wasn't sure he'd ever seen her smile. Ms. Beasley's husband had gone missing last year and to this day, never returned to the streets of Canton. Most folks just figured he'd run away with another woman but a few in town clung to the belief that he'd gotten lost during the hunting trip he'd supposed to have been on and died out there somewhere in the woods. It didn't really matter. The woman he'd left behind was a broken and shattered wreck either way.

"Where's Warren?" Megan asked.

"He had to hit the head," Robbie answered as Mrs. Ammon approached their booth.

"So what'll it be tonight, guys?" She smiled at them.

"Chili fries and a glass of sweet tea," Megan said without any hesitation whatsoever.

Robbie smirked, knowing that he'd been right how pointless it was for Megan to even be holding a menu, much less reading it. She got the same thing every time they were here, like clockwork.

"I'd like a double stacked burger please," Brently said. "And a vanilla coke."

"Do you want fries with that?" Mrs. Ammon grinned.

Brently shook his head. "No thank you, ma'am."

"And what about you boys?" Mrs. Ammon glanced at him and Pete as Robbie realized despite the trek through the woods that he wasn't really hungry.

"Just an iced water for me," Robbie told her.

"Now, Robbie. . ." Mrs. Ammon looked down her nose at him with an expression of concern. They were such regular customers that if something happened and they didn't always have enough cash to eat, she took care of them.

"Really," Robbie met her eyes. "I'm just not hungry tonight. That's all."

"Well I am," Pete spoke up loudly. "I'll take a full out breakfast platter with eggs, sausage, bacon, gravy, and biscuits with a triple side of hashbrowns."

Mrs. Ammon chuckled. "I think we can do

that."

She looked at Robbie again and asked, "You're sure?"

"I'm sure," he promised.

Mrs. Ammon left to take their order to her husband in the kitchen. Robbie watched her go. He was always impressed by the fact the husband and wife team worked the diner like they did. Surely, they had enough money to hire more help if they wanted to but they didn't. Outside of Warren's mother, a cleaning lady, and a back up cook, there were no other staff.

"Hey! Honey! Come here!" the gruff stranger sitting next to the main window shouted at Mrs. Ammon when she emerged from the kitchen after handing off the top page of the notepad in her hand.

"Wonder what he wants?" Pete whispered to Robbie. "There's already food in front of him."

Leave it to Pete to be looking out for everyone. Robbie shrugged. If Pete was worried about the man mistreating Mrs. Ammon, there was no need to be. Mr. Ammon wouldn't let that happen.

Everyone's attention was on the stranger in his trucker's cap and Mrs. Ammon.

"What is that thing out there?" The stranger pointed through the window at something on the other side of the diner's parking lot near where they'd come out of the woods.

Mrs. Ammon leaned forward, her eyes

squinting.

"I don't see anything," she said, straightening up. "I'm sorry."

"Name's Joe," the stranger told her. "And I'm sorry to say this, lady, but you gotta be blind. There's something right at the edge of those trees over there. Something big. You got bears around here?"

"Bears?" Mrs. Ammon's expression was more than a little incredulous. "I don't think so. Not that would come this close to the diner while there are lights on."

Joe flinched and then jumped out of his seat, pointing out the window again. "Do you see that!?!?"

Ms. Beasley had been ignoring the two of them as best she could, just sitting at the counter, picking at the food on her plate. She'd turned around as Joe leapt up though. The scream that came out of her was like nothing Robbie ever heard before. It was primal. . . pure terror given life.

The bathroom door opened. Warren walked out and froze in his tracks as some*thing* crashed through the diner's main window. Glass flew in every direction. Mrs. Ammon screamed too as a shard of it sliced a cut along the side of her cheek.

Whatever the thing was that came through the window, it wasn't a bear. The beast landed with a loud thud on the diner's floor right between Warren and the trucker, Joe, standing up on two legs like a man. It was easily eight feet tall, maybe taller. The beast's head was almost scraping the ceiling. Yellow eyes burned with rage as the beast looked at Joe and then turned its head around at Warren.

"Get out of there!" Megan yelled, tears forming in her eyes.

Warren never had a chance though. The beast grabbed hold of Warren, lifting him from the floor with a single hand. Joe slipped a large knife out of his boot and plunged it deep in the beast's back. Keeping its hold on Warren, the beast backhanded the trucker, knocking him out the window it had entered through.

Mr. Ammon charged from the kitchen carrying the shotgun all the locals knew he kept on hand in case there was ever trouble. Mrs. Ammon was rushing to him, blocking his line of fire.

Claws sunk into Warren. His eyes bulged as blood exploded from his throat where they'd entered. With a downward jerk of its hand, the beast opened Warren up from his neck to his groin. Entrails dumped out of his body, splattering wetly onto the diner floor. His body went limp in the beast's grasp as it raised the red drenched claws of the hand that killed him to its mouth, tongue flicking out to taste the blood on them.

Everything was utter chaos now. Mr. Ammon shoved his wife on by him into the kitchen. Pete had gotten up, snatching a chair from a table near their booth to use as a weapon, and was racing towards the monster. Yes, monster. Robbie figured that was the best name to describe the beast that his mind could come up with. Megan and Brently were out of their seats too. She had placed herself between Brently and the monster, her pocket knife out, blade open and ready. For his part, Robbie managed to get up too but that was it. He stood frozen, standing there helpless, his gaze glued to the monster and its rage.

With a thunderous roar, the monster hurled itself at Mr. Ammon. His shotgun boomed, blowing a chunk of meat from the monster's shoulder. Then Pete appeared between them, swinging the chair in his hands with all the strength his adrenaline flooded system could muster. The chair smashed into the monster's face, breaking apart as it made contact. If the monster hadn't been mad before, it sure as hell was now. Claws flashed through the air and blood flew as they tore away the entire left side of Pete's face.

"Pete!" Robbie heard himself cry as if he were outside of his own body, watching it from afar.

Mr. Ammon's shotgun boomed again. The monster stumbled as its blast blew a gaping hole in its side. Howling, the monster sprang forward, tearing the weapon from his hands. Mr. Ammon cried out as his trigger finger was bent backwards and ripped away with it. That cry was abruptly silenced as one of the monster's overly large hands closed over his face, their vice like grip crunching the bone of his skull inward. Rivers of red ran down his neck and over his chest as Mr. Ammon's body twitched like he was having a seizure. A final whimper escaped his body with his last breath.

The trucker, Joe, never came back inside. Robbie didn't know if the monster's blow had killed him, knocked him unconscious, or if Joe had just made a run for it. It wasn't as if he really knew any of them.

Robbie, still staring at the monster, figured out what it was. It had to be a Sasquatch. The height, the hair, its primate-like appearance. . . Not that the knowledge helped him any or gave him any kind of edge over it.

"We've gotta get out of here!" Brently shouted as Mrs. Ammon came tearing from the kitchen, a large knife raised in her right hand. The Sasquatch dropped her husband's corpse as she attacked it. The blade of her knife sunk deep into the meat of its chest. The knife broke where its blade touched its hilt as she tried to twist it inside the Sasquatch's body. The Sasquatch was hurting. Its movements were slowing and the glow of its burning, yellow eyes wasn't as bright. Robbie guessed the hulking beast was bleeding out from the wounds Mr. Ammon's shotgun had dealt it. Still, its growing weakness wasn't enough to save Mrs. Ammon. Her neck snapped, breaking, as the Sasquatch's hair-covered fingers closed around it. Slinging her corpse around like a ragdoll, the Sasquatch smashed Mrs. Ammon into the counter, the floor, and then finally flung her on top of a nearby table which gave way beneath her weight, its wood shattering and splintering.

"This way!" Robbie heard Megan yell to him. He turned to see that she had broken out the closest section of the diner's window and was shoving Brently through it.

The Sasquatch growled but there was as much pain as anger in the sound now. It took a step forward and careened sideways into the diner's counter. Robbie didn't wait to see if the Sasquatch recovered its balance. He hurried after Megan and Brently. Both of them had already gone through the broken window and were outside in the parking lot. Robbie jumped for it and crashed hard on the pavement of the lot with a grunt. His shoulder took the brunt of his landing but didn't break or get dislocated. It was going to have one hell of a bruise though. Small pieces of glass pricked the palms of his hands as he rolled over to scramble up onto his feet.

Robbie could hear the Sasquatch still stumbling around inside the diner as Megan and Brently ran for the road. There was a pair of headlights in the distance, coming up the road in the direction of the diner. He hoped to God that whoever it was would stop and help them.

****

After their visit with Paul at the newspaper office, Sheriff Bernard had considered heading to the station but opted not to. He and Deputy Miller, who sat in the patrol car's passenger seat next to him, had been running around all day. Both of them needed food and a break. When he suggested dropping by Ammon's Diner to grab some food and coffee, Deputy Miller was all in for it.

It was not long after sunset as their patrol car sped along the road to the diner. There wasn't any traffic but that didn't worry Bernard. Canton was a quiet town at this time of day. The teenagers and drinkers weren't really out and about yet while most of the working folk were already home for the night, eating dinner, helping kids with homework, and getting ready for the next day. Besides, Canton's one bar, its shopping center, and movie theatre were all on the other side of town. Ammon's Diner had set up business where it was, not so much for the townsfolk but for the truckers that passed through the region on a daily basis. Ammon's Diner and Lawson's gas station were truthfully the only two things that were close to the Interstate exit out here.

"Sheriff!" Miller cried out, pointing at the road.

Bernard blinked, sucking in a startled gasp, as he slammed the patrol car's brakes to the floorboard. The wheels shrieked in protest as Miller was flung forward despite her seatbelt, nearly smashing her face on the dash before the belt finally caught and snapped her back upright in her seat. Bernard fought with the steering wheel, trying to keep the car from turning sideways.

The patrol car came to a screeching halt just short of the kids in the road. The three kids had come out of seemingly nowhere, directly into their path. It was a minor miracle that Bernard managed not to run them over. Relief at that fact hit him first but was almost instantly replaced by righteous anger. From the looks of them, the kids were all damn old enough to know better than to run into the middle of the fragging road, especially with a car coming. There was no way in hell the group of them hadn't seen the patrol car's headlights.

Deputy Miller's seatbelt clicked loose as she

threw the passenger side door open and bolted from the car. She looked even more upset than he was. Miller's gun cleared her holster, though she didn't directly aim the weapon at the group of teenagers, as she marched towards a young girl with long, blonde hair tied into a tight ponytail.

"What the hell do y'all think you're doing?" Miller barked.

"Help!" the girl Sheriff Bernard now recognized as Megan Drake shouted. "There's a monster in the diner!"

"It killed Mr. and Mrs. Ammon!" a chubby, geeky kid added.

Bernard didn't need to hear anything more. He threw the patrol car into drive again and cut around Deputy Miller and the kids, flicking on its sirens. Something told him that whatever the kids were claiming to be in the diner was the same thing that had killed the four men in the woods. The car bounced as he took it over the side of the road and into the diner's parking lot. All the lights inside the diner were still on. Its main window was broken but that wasn't what caught Bernard's attention. That was consumed by the over eight foot tall beast, moving on two legs like a man. Glass exploded outward as the beast smashed through another section of the window, leaping into the parking lot. Bernard could see that it was wounded. Its movements were unsteady and awkward. Even so, with its size and strength, the beast was still something that he wasn't going to mess around with.

As the creature ran forward to meet his patrol car, Bernard floored the gas to meet it. The car crashed, head on, into the massive beast. Its hood folded up in front of him before the impact sent the beast flying backwards. It thudded onto the pavement of the lot, landing face up, and lay there, unmoving. A puddle of red was forming about its hair-covered body as Bernard shook his head to clear it and stumbled out of the badly damaged car. The smell of leaking gas worried him as he heard Deputy Miller and the kids running in his direction from the road.

"Don't!" Bernard warned them. "Stay back!"

From where he stood, Bernard could see that the beast was still breathing. Its chest rose and fell in an uneven rhythm. His gut told him that the thing was more than just knocked out, it was dying. Bernard realized that he had instinctively drawn his .44 Magnum. The weight of the heavy revolver in his hand was reassuring and helped him focus.

Deputy Miller had stopped as he'd called out to her and was now holding position, halfway between the road and the diner, keeping the kids back too.

Moving forward cautiously, Bernard approached the beast. Any doubt that Bigfoot was real left him because he was certainly looking at one right now. There wasn't anything else the hulking, hairy creature could be.

The Sasquatch's eyes flickered open, its black lips parting another moan. Bernard aimed for the thing's forehead and fired. The bullet from his .44 struck the Sasquatch dead center there, just above its yellow eyes. Skull bone cracked, caving inward, as blood and brain matter exploded outward. The Sasquatch jerked as the bullet entered and then never moved again.

Certain the Sasquatch was truly dead, his attention turned to the body of a man lying on the pavement just outside the diner. He was dead too, neck bent and twisted about at an unnatural angle. Bernard didn't recognize the man but it was plain that the poor bastard was a trucker who just happened to have stopped for a bite to eat at the wrong time. There wasn't anything he could do for him.

Sheriff Bernard moved closer to the diner, peering inside, to see the blood smeared counter and the bodies scattered about on the floor. Two of them were kids like the ones that had come running onto the road. Mr. and Mrs. Ammon were there too. There was smoke pouring out of the diner's kitchen. Bernard had seen enough. He retreated from the diner to where his patrol car sat. It was too trashed to likely ever be drivable again but Bernard didn't care about that. Sure, the paperwork would

72

suck, hardcore, but what he wanted from the car right now was in its trunk. He popped it and shouldered the heavy gear bag inside. Leaving the trunk open, Bernard jogged across the parking lot to where Deputy Miller and the kids were waiting.

****

Deputy Clarkson pulled into the lot outside the station. It had been a fragging long day. All he wanted to do was clock out and go home but there was no hope of that. Deputies Gillan and Russell hadn't returned from the errand he'd dispatched them on yet. Hell, he hadn't even been able to reach them by radio or cell for hours. Not wanting to send anyone else after them, as the manpower couldn't be spared, Clarkson had returned to the station in hopes that he would catch a lucky break. Sometimes, Steph, their best dispatcher, knew things that the rest of the department didn't. He prayed this was one of those times and maybe Gillan and Russell were just still out of range or there was some sort of interference with the signal at the worksite he'd sent them to.

Steph's car was the only other one parked in the station's lot. Sheriff Bernard wasn't back yet. That struck Clarkson as odd and worried him as he walked up the short set of steps leading to the station's front door. As he swung it inward,

Clarkson heard Steph give a startled cry.

"Dang it, Henry!" she yelled at him from her desk, cheeks flushed a hot red. "You nearly scared me to death!"

"Sorry," Clarkson apologized. He hated it when folks used his first name but didn't remind Steph of it. She had been pretty badly spooked by his sudden appearance so he couldn't blame her for screwing up this time. "Where's everyone else?"

Steph glared at him. "How am I supposed to know? Brent and Rigdon are the only people who have answered me on the radio in a while now. What the devil is going on out there anyway?"

"Hell if I know," Clarkson shrugged. "Honestly, I had been hoping you could tell me."

"Well I don't know much," Steph said. "Brent and Rigdon are still out there keeping Harley Road blocked. Last I heard from the Sheriff, he and Deputy Miller were stopping to get something to eat on the way in. And I haven't heard squat from Russell and Gillan since their radio cut out."

Clarkson raised an eyebrow. "What do you mean cut out?"

"Gillan had called in, said she and Russell had found more bodies at that worksite you and the sheriff sent them to. Apparently, the whole crew up there had been killed. That was the last word I got from her. After that, there was a strange burst of static but then nothing else. I tried to radio her back but got no answer. I figured something happened to their car's radio from the sound of things," Steph told him.

"Why didn't you radio me to let me know?" Clarkson pressed her.

"Look now," Steph got up and came around her desk at him. "You try dealing with all the calls that have been coming in all freaking day by yourself and see how you handle it, Mr. Senior Deputy!"

"Whoa," Clarkson held his hands up at his waist, palms out, in a gesture of surrender. "Take it easy, Steph."

"I swear Sheriff Bernard really needs to hire some more help around here," Steph grumbled.

That was when he noticed that though the ringer was muted, the lights for the various lines on the phone that sat on Steph's desk were all flashing.

"Steph. . ." Clarkson stared at her. "What's going on out there?"

"You'd think it was Halloween," Steph huffed. "Seems like everyone in town and their cousin has seen some kind of monster. . . creeping around in the woods, running across the road or their lawn, heck, the last call I took though, it came from Matheson's Grocery."

"And?" Clarkson pressed.

"I was about to radio you about it when you came walking in," Steph snapped her hair about. "I would have written the call off like all the others but I got more than one call from the store. They all came in together, right at the same time. And that last one. . . it was from Richard."

"The store owner," he commented.

"Yeah," Steph nodded. "He sounded deadly serious and more than a little scared but his story lined up with the ones of the other calls. Something big and hairy, he said, was in the woods around the store's parking lot. He didn't know what it was but the animal was driving his customers away."

"This day. . ." Clarkson shook his head and sighed.

"It's one for the record books," Steph agreed. "Everything's just. . .just crazy."

A moment passed before either of them spoke again. Finally Steph said, "So what are you going to do about the call from the store?"

"I want you to get on the radio and find the sheriff. Let him know about all this craziness A.S.A.P. Then I want you to send whoever else you can reach to the store. I may need back up there," Clarkson ordered.

"You're going back out?" Steph asked. "I thought you'd be on your way home. Your shift's over, you know?"

Clarkson sucked in a deep breath before

answering. "I can't head home yet. Not until I've at least checked things out at the general store and you get in touch with the sheriff."

He walked towards the back of the department.

"Where you going?" Steph called after him, confused.

Clarkson didn't answer.

"Deputy!" Steph raised her voice.

A few minutes later, Clarkson passed by her desk, this time heading out of the station. He was carrying an AR-15 with a drum magazine attached to its underside. There was a pump action shotgun slung over his shoulder by its strap and he was wearing a second pistol, holstered to his hip, opposite his usual Sig Sauer P226.

Steph's eyes bugged at the sight of him. "Damn, Clarkson."

It wasn't like her to swear so Clarkson knew just how ready to fight a war he must look.

"You just find the sheriff and get me some back up to that store A.S.A.P," he ordered.

"Will do," Steph promised.

"I'm locking up on my way out, Steph," Clarkson added. "Don't you open that door for anyone that's not wearing a badge, you got me?"

She nodded.

"Anyone or anything else comes knocking, you get a gun out the armory back there and. . ."

Clarkson went on.

"I got it," Steph nodded again.

Stopping at the door, with it halfway open, Clarkson looked at Steph one final time. "If I'm not back in a couple of hours and the sheriff isn't either, I want you to get yourself a gun and the hell out of town. Take the spare patrol car in the rear lot. It's a lot tougher and faster than that little Toyota you drive."

"You really think things are that bad out there?" Steph was getting more freaked out every second.

"I do," Clarkson answered. "Call it a feeling in my gut but I really do. You'll be safe here with the place locked up long enough for me to go to check things out and if I don't make it. . ."

"Clarkson, I hope you've just lost your bloody marbles," Steph told him, not holding her feelings back. "But you be careful out there."

He gave her a sharp nod and slammed the door behind him as he stepped out.

****

The explosion lit up the night. It was like something out of a big budget action movie. Orange and red hues of flame shot upwards into the dark sky above Ammon's Diner. The windows that were still intact burst out, spraying shards of glass like fletchettes. Bits of wood and metal flew like shrapnel. The blossoming flames licked out into the parking lot, lighting the closest car ablaze.

"Holy fragging Hell," Brently muttered.

The kid's words were exactly what Sheriff Bernard was feeling watching the diner burn. It was all so surreal. The diner had been a fixture of the town as long as he could remember. He'd eaten there countless times, known the Ammons well. He stared into the raging fire for a moment longer and then shook his head. If only he and Miller had gotten there sooner maybe. . .somehow. . . they could have saved the folks who had died in there.

"There wasn't anyone alive in there," Sheriff Bernard said more to himself than the others with him. On the edge of the road, looking across the parking lot, and the fire were a trio of teenage kids and his deputy, Miller. The kids had fled from the diner when the Sasquatch attacked it but he was the last one to get a glimpse inside the place. He remembered the bodies scattered about its floor, the blood smeared and splattered over its counter and walls.

As if reading his mind, Miller spoke up. "We've got bigger things to worry about, sir."

Her words brought Bernard out of his thoughts and his attention to the present. Bernard turned his head around towards Miller.

"That thing's dead," he assured her. "Just look over there. Its body is burning."

As if to accentuate his claim, at that moment, his patrol car blew. The flames from the bits of wood flung out from the diner managed to ignite its gas tank.

"That's not what I'm talking about," Miller inclined her head in the direction of the trees across the road. Sheriff Bernard followed her gaze. There was something in the woods, something big.

"You've got to be kidding me," Bernard griped.

"If there's one. . ." Miller said and then added, "Nothing exists in a vacuum, you know?"

"Frag it," Bernard knew she was right. It just made sense. If Sasquatch was real, there sure as hell had to be more than just the one he had killed. The question Bernard wasn't sure he wanted an answer to was just how many of them were around the town of Canton.

"We can't stay here. We're too exposed," Bernard commented, his eyes scanning the parking lot of the burning diner. All of the cars in the lot had been parked right up to the building and weren't viable.

"I'm open to suggestions on how to change that," Miller frowned.

"Ma'am," the teenage girl spoke up. "Our friend, Warren, his house is just over the hill."

Sheriff Bernard tried to know as many of Canton's residents as he could. He recognized the girl. Her name was Megan . . .and he knew Warren too. That kid was trouble. He very likely would have ended up in jail if his life hadn't been cut short this evening.

"That's not a bad idea," Bernard grinned. "His mom owns a car but usually walks to work and back. Isn't that right?"

Megan nodded her head. "Yes sir. She wasn't working tonight so she's likely there waiting on Warren to come home."

Tears welled up in Megan's eyes but she quickly wiped them away and kept herself from sobbing.

"Do you need us to show you how to get there?" a chubby kid named Brently asked.

"I know the way," Sheriff Bernard answered more gruffly than he meant to, making Brently flinch. "We'd best get moving."

Sheriff Bernard paused only long enough to fling the bag he'd gotten from his patrol car onto the ground and unzip it. He thrust a shotgun up into Miller's hands then produced an AR-15 for himself from the bag. Shoving an extra magazine into the pocket of his pants, Bernard left the rest of the bag where it lay and started walking along the road at a brisk pace. His gut told him that cutting through the woods in the dark would be a very bad idea. The thing that had been watching them from the trees across the road seemed to be gone but he had no idea where to and that worried him. He figured it was a hell of a lot safer to take the road and walk a bit farther. On the road at least, they might have a chance to see or hear a Sasquatch if it came at them. The woods were where those things lived. Their eyes were better adapted to the dark and Bernard didn't doubt that they could move with such stealth among the trees, that someone would be dead before they even knew the group was being attacked.

Their luck held. Whatever kept the Sasquatch from attacking them in the diner's parking lot was still working for them. They reached the end of the driveway leading up to Warren and his mom's trailer without incident. Bernard hoped that meant it was only a single beast that was stalking them and that there was safety in numbers. There was five of them counting the three kids. That was the best theory Bernard had as to why they hadn't been attacked already.

Sheriff Bernard paused looking up the driveway. The car they were after was there, a beat up old Toyota that had seen far better days. He knew it ran though. He'd heard its rough sounding engine around town earlier in the week.

"It appears there's no one home up there," Miller gestured at the trailer.

She was right. There were no lights on inside of it. Bernard squinted in the darkness, focusing in on the trailer's front door, realizing that it wasn't fully shut. He shook his head.

Megan took off running up the drive, calling out, "Ms. Hawk! Ms. Hawk, are you in there?"

"Damn it," Bernard heard Miller swear under her breath before running after the kid.

Bernard whirled on the two teenage boys, stopping them from following. "Don't even think about it!"

As Megan drew closer to the trailer's front door, she slowed down. Miller came up behind her, grabbing Megan by her right shoulder. The girl's head whipped around at Miller.

"We've got to make sure she's okay," Megan said. "I mean, we can't just steal her car, ya know?"

"We do, but that's up to us, not you, kid," Miller told her.

Megan scowled at Miller and looked up towards the trailer again.

"We don't need anybody else getting killed," Miller frowned. "Get back down there with the others. I'll check out the trailer."

Bernard knew Miller wasn't going to like whatever was waiting for her inside the place. No one had ever answered Megan's calls so that most likely meant Warren's mother was dead already. Still, he left dealing with the trailer and Megan to her. Bernard trusted Miller's instincts and toughness.

"Don't you need to go up there and get the keys?" Brently asked as Bernard quietly popped the Toyota's door open and slid into the driver's seat.

Bernard cut his eyes at the kid with a smug expression. He dislodged the plastic cover of the steering column and found the wiring harness connector beneath it. The wires he needed ran straight up the length of the column. He pulled aside the bundle that contained those for the battery, ignition, and starter wire. The battery wire was almost always red in color. Bernard spotted it easily even in the dimness of the starlight that was coming through the forward window above him. He began to strip about an inch of insulation from the battery wire and when he was done, twisted them together. Ever so carefully, Bernard connected the battery wire to the ignition on/off wire. He smiled as the dash lights came on inside the car. Now all he needed to do was spark the starter wire and rev the engine. Well, other than breaking the steering lock but that could wait.

Brently and Robbie stood watching him work the entire time, mesmerized by how easy he made it look.

Meanwhile, Deputy Miller stepped between Megan and the trailer. The girl was right. They couldn't just take the car and leave. She had told Megan to get down to where the boys were. Megan wouldn't move though. Miller couldn't believe it but she was starting to really like the girl. She could see her younger self in Megan.

The only light was that of the stars and the weak, pale moon above. It was enough to see that the door of the trailer was cracked open but that was it. Miller flicked on the flashlight that was mounted to the side of her shotgun. Its beam was bright and cut through the darkness like a knife. Miller aimed the light at the trailer door and heard Megan suck in a startled breath from behind her. Beneath the door, the step going into the trailer was stained red with blood and it was a set of smashed human fingers keeping the door open at its bottom, wedged there and unmoving.

"Frag!" Miller grumbled.

"Do you think. . .?" Megan said in a voice that was barely louder than a whisper.

"I told you to get to the car, girl!" Miller barked. "Now!"

Megan finally listened to her, darting down the drive away from the trailer as Miller started forward. She advanced on the partly open door slowly, her shotgun at the ready. Sweat beaded on her forehead. Miller knew just how damn strong and fast a Sasquatch was. She'd seen enough to know that you didn't screw around with the things. One mistake and you'd be dead.

Reaching the door, Miller's nose twitched at the horrid smell leaking out from the trailer's interior. She gagged at the scent but kept her focus. The smell was that of a heavy animal musk mixed with rotting flesh. The fingers caught in the door still hadn't moved. She made up her mind right then and there that the person they belonged to had to be dead. Even if they weren't, she couldn't afford to take the chance to check when only God knew what was waiting on her inside the trailer. She backpedaled, retreating from the door as slowly as she'd approached it.

Miller heard the engine of the Toyota in the driveway turn over and roar to life. Her lips parted slightly in a wry smirk knowing it was the sheriff who had surely hotwired the car.

"Come on, Miller!" he shouted at her.

The kids had piled into the backseat. It was cramped with all three of them there. Miller raced down the drive and hopped into the Toyota's passenger seat.

"Warren's mom?" Bernard asked her, already knowing what the answer would be.

"Dead," Miller confirmed. "We need to get out of here before we're next."

"Right," Bernard shifted gears and punched the gas. Gravel flew as the little Toyota rocketed in reverse down the drive, bouncing onto the main road.

****

Brent and Rigdon had been closer to the store than Clarkson when Steph's call for backup there came over the radio. They'd been at the store for nearly two minutes now by Rigdon's internal clock. He was crouched down, hiding behind the hood of their patrol car, staring at Brent's head on the pavement not more than three yards from him. The big man's eyes were wide open in a look of intense shock and pain. Blood dripped from Brent's open mouth. Neither of them had any idea what to expect when they arrived at the store and had paid the price for it.

Their patrol car had come swerving from the road into the store's parking lot with the sirens going full blast. Something had apparently knocked out the power in the area because the lights in the lot and inside the store were both out. It wasn't fully dark though. A pickup truck was burning brightly at the other end of the lot from where they'd entered and a few small fires looked to be going within the store as well. Rigdon's mind couldn't process what he was seeing. There were bodies everywhere, strewn all over the parking lot. He felt the patrol car drive over one and the crunch of bone. It was all like a scene out of some kind of apocalypse movie where society had collapsed, falling apart at the seams impossibly fast. There was no question as to the cause of it all though. Rigdon's eyes first caught sight of the largest of the three creatures sitting near the store's entrance, holding a woman's leg up to its blood-smeared mouth, gnawing away on it. The other two were spread out. One was standing near the burning pick up, seemingly watching it burn while the other, hearing their sirens and seeing the car's headlights, was making a beeline straight for them, thickly muscled, hair-covered legs pumping with all the speed the thing could muster. . . and that was a hell of a lot. Brent slammed on the brakes, stopping the car before the hulking beast reached it. The big deputy leaped out of the car, drawing the .45 caliber, 1911 holstered on his hip. The pistol boomed in rapid succession, Brent aiming it in a two-handed grip. Rigdon saw the big deputy's rounds striking the monster. A round smacked into the thing's shoulder, several more struck its chest, but none of them so much as slowed the monster down. Brent was still firing into it as the monster reached him. Rigdon watched in horror as the beast grabbed Brent by the sides of his head and ripped it from the big deputy's shoulders in an explosion of blood. Flinging the passenger side door open, Rigdon hurled himself out of the patrol car. He hit the ground low and stayed down. In the distance, someone was screaming. It drew the monster's attention and

Rigdon heard the heavy footfalls of its feet thudding away. Getting himself together as best he could, Rigdon pressed his back against the patrol car, hiding behind the door he'd opened.

Rigdon's breath came in ragged gasps. He was terrified out of his mind. His mind was still reeling from the insanity of the mess he was in. A monster had just ripped his partner's head off and tossed it onto the ground. The world didn't seem real anymore. It was as if he had suddenly been plunged into a horror film come to life. There was no training for what he was dealing with now and there were dozens of dead bodies all around him through the parking lot including Brent's headless corpse. Rigdon was literally trembling. Knowing he couldn't stay where he was and that it was going to take a lot more firepower than the Glock in his holster to stop the monsters, Rigdon leaned into the patrol car, reaching over to pop its trunk. He heard it spring open and still keeping low, crawled on his hands and knees next to the car towards it.

Apparently, there were a few customers and employees from the store left alive and they were the only things keeping him alive at the moment. It was his job to protect them but that was a fragging joke. Figuring it would take a minor miracle just to keep himself from being torn apart by the monsters, Rigdon reached the trunk of the patrol car. His right hand slinked up into

it, probing about in search of the bag stored there.
His fingers closed on the bag and Rigdon slid it
out of the trunk. He was careful to be as quiet
as he could, praying with his whole heart that the
monsters would continue not to notice him.
Inside the bag was a standard issue, pump action
12 gauge. Rigdon took it out and checked to
make sure it was loaded like it was supposed to
be. Seeing that it was, he slowly worked its
pump, trying to minimize the noise made by the
action, chambering a round. From his position
he couldn't see any of the three monsters now.
Rigdon hoped they were the only three but there
was no way to know that for sure. There could
be even more of the monsters inside the store or
in the woods surrounding the parking lot.

The angry growl of a monster, too close, sent
Rigdon crawling the rest of the way around the
patrol car. He stopped at the driver's door which
was still open from where Brent had leapt out.
And that's where he still sat, staring into the wide
open, now lifeless eyes of Brent's head. Rigdon
heard the monster give a loud grunt and could
tell it was on the other side of the patrol car from
where he sat. His knuckles went white as he
clutched the pump action shotgun even tighter.
Time was running out for him. He couldn't stay
hidden when there wasn't really anywhere to hide.
Besides, he was supposed to the hero for the
story, wasn't he? It was his job to be saving

anyone here that the beasts hadn't killed yet, not sat here cowering and shaking in his boots. Taking a deep breath, Rigdon steadied himself and got ready to start doing his job. Before he could spring up to his feet and start blasting away at the monsters though the blaring sound of sirens froze him where he was.

The patrol car roared into the parking lot outside the general store. Whoever was driving it slammed on the brakes. Its tires screeched as the car came to an abrupt halt. Rigdon's eyes went wide as he saw Senior Deputy Clarkson get out of the vehicle. Two of the monsters were already bounding towards him. Clarkson hefted an AR-15 with a drum magazine from the car and turned to meet them. The senior deputy stood his ground, opening fire. God only knew how many rounds he poured into the closest beast and then the other but they sent blood and gore flying. The two monsters collapsed, twitching in pools of their own blood where they fell.

"Rigdon! That you, son?" Clarkson yelled at him. "I could use a fragging hand!"

Stumbling onto his feet, Rigdon saw the last of the three beasts coming across the parking lot at the senior deputy. He jerked up his shotgun, bracing the weapon against his shoulder, and fired. The shotgun boomed. His shot blew open the beast's side in a spray of blood and entrails. The beast roared, spinning about, its yellow eyes locking in on him. Rigdon worked the pump of his shotgun, chambering another round. Seeing he wasn't going to have time to get off a second shot, Rigdon decided to get the hell out of the beast's path. He leaped onto the hood of his patrol car, sliding across it. His feet landed on the pavement and he ducked there, using the car as cover, so that he'd be out of Clarkson's line of fire. The chatter of Clarkson's AR-15 was deafening. Rounds that missed the beast whizzed over Rigdon's head as he kept down. The beast was howling, squealing, in pain before it finally collapsed with a loud thud onto the pavement of the parking lot.

"Rigdon!" Clarkson called out. "You still breathing?"

"Yeah!" Rigdon shouted.

He stood up from where he was crouching. Clarkson was staring at him.

"I see Brent didn't make it," the senior deputy grunted. "Too bad. He was a good officer."

Rigdon almost wondered if Clarkson was implying that he wasn't. He and Clarkson had certainly had some rough moments in the past.

As they stood there, a small crowd of survivors from the attack in the store were emerging from their hiding places. Some of them were pretty banged up. All of them were scared out of their minds, faces pale, and eyes full of shock.

"Crap," Clarkson muttered under his breath as he looked over the crowd.

The senior deputy closed into whisper range with him. "We can't do squat for them. Things like the ones we just killed are rampaging all over town."

Rigdon swallowed hard at that news.

"We can't just leave them either," he found himself arguing.

Clarkson sighed and shook his head in frustration.

"Okay everybody!" the senior deputy yelled. "Y'all need to know that those monsters, or whatever the hell they are, they aren't alone. There are more of them out there."

"So what are you going to do about it?" a burly redneck guy in the crowed challenged Clarkson.

"Yeah!" another voice in the crowd called out. "One of those things trashed my car! I can't even get home!"

"My kids are home all by themselves, Deputy!" a woman's voice shrieked.

Rigdon was terrified they were about to lose any control their badges gave them over the motley crowd when Clarkson pointed his AR-15 upwards and let a burst fly into the dark clouds above. That shut everyone up quick.

"Look, the thing is there ain't a hell of a lot we

can do for you right now! Hell, I don't even have a clue what shape the town's ambulances and hospital are in, people," Clarkson told them honestly. "My suggestion is that all of you get home as fast as you can, lock your doors, get out your guns if you've got one, and hold tight until you hear otherwise!"

"That's a load of crap!" the redneck spat. "Ain't it your job to protect us?"

Rigdon was stunned as Clarkson leveled the barrel of his AR at the redneck.

"Yeah, it is," Clarkson snarled. "But right now, sir," the senior deputy said the word like an insult, "you're going to shut the hell up and do what I say. Get the frag into your vehicle. . ."

"One of those things smashed it to crap!" the redneck protested.

"Then find someone to get a ride with and get the hell out of here," Clarkson raged. "We can't protect you folks! There are only two of us here! Now everybody get home and stay there!"

Clarkson fired another burst into the air to hammer what he was saying into the heads of the folks in the crowd. Those that could scattered, running for their cars and trucks. Those without a vehicle either caught whatever ride they could or ran off on foot. The wounded, those alone, were merely left where they were.

"Damn," Rigdon stared at the senior deputy. "There's going to be hell to pay for that later if we survive tonight."

"It's on me, not you, son," Clarkson assured him, "And it had to be done. You know I'm right. There was no other option. More of those things could come through here any minute. Even if we got everyone into that store and tried to fortify the place, they'd get in. It'd just be another massacre."

Rigdon couldn't argue with Clarkson. Everything the senior deputy said made sense. He still didn't like it but there wasn't anything he could do about it.

"What about us?" Ridgon asked. "What are we going to do?"

"Find the sheriff, regroup and then, son," Clarkson grinned, "we're going to war."

****

Sheriff Bernard, Miller, and the kids got out of the patrol car. The lot outside of the department was clear of the beasts and there was no sign of them lurking in the woods about it, at least that they could see. The drive through town had been like a trip through a madman's violent and bloody nightmare. It had ripped out his heart and left Bernard feeling like crap. The Sasquatch really were just about everywhere in the town. People were dying. People were dying on his watch. Bernard told himself that if they'd stopped to help any of them, they would be too and would have accomplished nothing in the grand scheme of things. He didn't know if that was really true or merely a lie to make him feel better so that he could stay in the fight. What he did know was that they had a hell of a lot more firepower than what they were carrying and a plan. Heading to the department was the best first step that either he or Miller could come up with. The building was built to withstand an attack and he kept the armory stocked beyond what regulations really allowed. And though he'd been putting off trying to ask for outside help, mostly because Bernard didn't think anyone would believe him about what was happening here in Canton, that was the first damn thing he planned on doing once they were all inside the department.

Miller looked at him. He inclined his head signaling her to get moving towards the department's front door. As she raced up the short set of steps, Bernard was still scanning the trees, waiting for one of the Sasquatches to come bursting out to attack them. Miller reached the door and turned there to provide cover for him and the rest of the group to join her.

"Not good," Miller commented as he slid by her to get at the department's door. It wasn't ever supposed to be locked up like this. The department didn't really close. Someone was there twenty-four -seven. It took Bernard a second to use the keypad beside the door and his key in order to get it open. When he did, Bernard stumbled through it with a start, not realizing that so much of his weight was braced against it. He was met by the barrel of an AR-15.

"Oh crap!" Steph shouted, swinging the gun out of his face.

Bernard's heart was pounding in his chest as he reached out, taking the weapon from Steph's hands.

"I am so sorry, sir," Steph told him, tears welling up in her eyes.

"Sshhh. . ." Bernard shushed her, shoving Steph back so that he could move deeper into the department and let the others in behind him.

Miller ushered Brently, Robbie, and Megan by her and then closed the department door, locking it. Her expression was grim as Bernard met her eyes but the news she had from him was good.

"Still looks clear out there," Miller told him.

"What's going on out there, Sheriff?" Steph sobbed. "All these reports of monsters kept pouring in all day and now. . . "

"Now what?" Bernard asked.

"Now, I can't reach anyone," Steph shook her head. "Not a single officer is responding to their radios and the phones are down."

Bernard cocked an eyebrow at that last bit.

He repeated her words just to be sure. "The phones are out?"

Steph nodded. "They went dead an hour ago. Power not long after. The generator kicked in but I've kept most of the lights off just in case. . . in case something out there might see them."

"Has anyone else been here?" Miller asked.

"Just Clarkson," Steph answered. "He came through earlier. There was a report of an attack at the general store. He ordered me to get in touch with anyone else I could and send them there then armed up like he was going to war and left. I haven't heard from him since then."

"Damn," Miller was shaking her head. "Guess things are even worse than we thought."

"I'd say," Bernard agreed.

"What the hell do we do now?" Brently wheezed. The chubby teenager appeared to be on the verge of having an anxiety attack or something. He was having trouble breathing.

"Settle down," Bernard told him. "Freaking out isn't going to help anything. We've all got to keep calm and stay focused or none of us will make it out of this mess alive."

"Yes sir," Brently answered weakly.

"You didn't answer me, Sheriff," Steph said. "How bad is it out there? What's really happening?"

Bernard grunted. "It's bad."

He paused for a second wondering if Steph

could handle the truth based on how frantic she already was. Bernard decided she could. Steph was a tough lady, had to be to be a dispatcher, so he said, "When we came through the main part of town, it was torn all to hell. God only knows how many of those monsters are out there. It's just as bad as all those calls you said came in must have made it sound."

Bernard watched Steph closely as his words sunk in.

Her face bunched up and then relaxed. "These monsters. . . what are they? Where did they come from?"

"They're Sasquatch," Miller answered before he could.

"What?" Steph smirked. "Seriously?"

"Seriously," Miller confirmed. "As to where they came from. . .?"

"I have a theory on that," Bernard said. "I think they've always been here around the town. Hell, there are a lot of stories about them, aren't there? Anyway, my bet is something stirred them up, ticked them off to the point that they decided we humans needed to be shown who this land really belongs to."

"That makes sense," Miller nodded.

"Does any of that matter?" Megan cut in. "Weren't you just saying we needed to stay focused?"

Bernard turned to look at the girl, impressed

by her. "Yeah, I was."

"Then what's the plan?" Megan demanded of him.

"We should be safe enough here for long enough to catch our breath," Bernard said. "So that's what we're going to do. While we're doing that, I'm going to see if I can get us some help."

"And I am going to get us loaded up with some real firepower," Miller smirked.

"Alright then," Bernard walked over to Megan, holding his shotgun out to her. "You ever used one of these?"

"I'm pretty sure I can figure it out," the spunky girl shrugged.

"I want you and your friends to stay here in this main room. There's food and such in the vending machines," Bernard managed a smile. "Smash'em open if you need to."

"Copy that," Megan laughed.

"The three of you get what rest you can but keep an eye on that door," Bernard ordered her. "If anything tries to get through it, blast the hell out of it. Deputy Miller and I will hear the gunfire and come running."

"Yes sir," Megan assured him.

Miller had already disappeared, heading for the armory.

Bernard turned back to Steph, "You stay with them."

Steph nodded.

Without another word, Bernard went into his office, shutting its door behind him. He pulled the shades down over the glass so he could be as alone as he could without any prying eyes or ears then sat at his desk. Placing his head into his hands, Bernard sat there wondering how in the hell things had gone so wrong, knowing that he'd done all he could and yet, still, the town he was supposed to protect was burning out there. Every minute that ticked by, more people were dying. He started praying. When he was finished, Bernard sucked in a deep breath, steeling himself against all the horrors that were likely still to come and reached for the radio on his desk. With the phones dead and his cell not working anymore either, it was his only option.

"This is Sheriff Bernard calling Buncombe 1, over?"

Only crackling static answered him.

"Repeat. This is Sheriff Bernard calling Buncombe 1, over?"

Bernard sighed, listening to the continuing static. Then he tried again.

"This is Sheriff Bernard of Canton, calling Jackson 1, over?"

No one in either of the neighboring counties were responding. Bernard didn't know if there was some sort of interference or if it was equip. He kept trying though for a solid five minutes before reaching the point where his words were a plea to anyone out there who might be listening. His shoulders slumping in defeat, Bernard gave up on the radio. If there was anyone who could hear him, they surely would have answered by now. He didn't even want to think about what the lack of an answer might mean. Bernard knew the two counties had their own Bigfoot stories and legends.

Getting up, Bernard walked over to the window of his office and peeped out through the closed blinds at the others. Miller still hadn't returned from the armory but everyone else was in the department's main room. Steph was making coffee. Megan sat in a chair facing the front door with the shotgun he had given her ready for anything that might try to come through it. Brently was munching away at candy bars and chips he had gotten from the vending machines. And the other kid, Robbie, he was standing next to Megan as if watching over her while she watched the door. Every single one of them was depending on him except he didn't have any answers. Forty-eight hours ago, Bernard never would have believed the crap they were caught up in now could even happen in the real world.

They were on their own and Bernard knew it. The best plan he had was to arm up and try to get them the hell out of town. If he was really lucky, maybe, just maybe, he could save some more folks on their way out.

****

Rigdon and Clarkson hung around in front of the general store long enough for the survivors of the attack there to clear out. The senior deputy paced back and forth, his AR-15 ready for anything that dared come out of the woods to challenge them. Rigdon administered what first aid he could to those who needed it though it ticked the senior deputy off to no end. It was either patch them up enough to get them up and going or leave them to die and he wasn't going to do that no matter what Clarkson said. When he had tended to the last of the wounded, Rigdon helped the woman whose arm he'd rigged a brace for into her car and got her headed home.

He could see that Clarkson wanted to tell him it was all a waste of time. Clarkson didn't though. Instead, he just motioned for Rigdon to take the driver's seat of his patrol car.

"Come on," Clarkson urged. "We need to get the hell out of here too! There's work to be done."

Rigdon cranked up the patrol car as Clarkson clutched his AR-15. The rifle was mounted with a one hundred and fifty round drum magazine. He had spent part of it during their battle with the beasts earlier but it was far from depleted.

"Where to?" Rigdon asked.

"Take us back to the department," Clarkson answered. "I left Steph there. Besides, if Bernard is still alive, that's where he will head for."

Rigdon nodded and got the car moving. As they sped along the road, all the lights were out. Not just those in the houses they passed but the streetlights as well. Something had knocked out the power. Rigdon didn't want to give the beasts credit for it. If it was those things, then that meant they were way more intelligent than he or anyone else had thought. That kind of cunning made them even more dangerous than their seemingly impossible strength and speed.

The patrol car's headlights cut the darkness of the night like gleaming knife blades. Rigdon's survival instinct told him to floor the gas, get to the department as fast as possible, but he knew better than that. Along the road were cars that had been attacked and left abandoned or smashed. He was forced to keep his speed low enough to be able to swerve around them. As careful as he was being, Rigdon still wasn't prepared when a huge, hulking monster came bursting out of the woods directly in front of the car. Rigdon spun the steering wheel hard to the left. The tires shrieked in protest at the sudden, sharp change in direction but he managed to dodge the Sasquatch.

"Frag!" Clarkson yelped, tossed about where he sat, only his seatbelt saving him from worse.

The patrol car sped by the Sasquatch. It wasn't done with them yet though. Thickly muscled, hair-covered legs pumped beneath the thing as it came chasing after them. The state of the road kept Rigdon from slamming the gas to the floor even then. He could see in the rearview that the monster was actually gaining on them.

"Can't you go any faster?" Clarkson yelled.

Rigdon tried and nearly crashed them into a van that turned halfway across the road. Sparks flew and metal screeched as the passenger side of the patrol car scraped against it.

"Watch it!" Clarkson raged.

Unable to take his eyes from the road ahead, Rigdon shouted, "I'm trying!"

The Sasquatch caught up to the patrol car. With a roar, the beast smashed its hands down onto the trunk. Its hairy fingers plunged through the metal. The beast came to a halt, attempting to stop the car through sheer brute force. The patrol car lurched as the Sasquatch almost succeeded. It might have if the lid of the trunk hadn't ripped free. The straining beast was sent reeling backwards as the car shot forward. Rigdon saw the top of the trunk spinning into the trees that ran along the side of the road.

"That was. . ." Clarkson started. He didn't

get to finish though. Another Sasquatch charged out of the trees, slamming into the car. The driver's door folded inward, its window shattering. Rigdon screamed as shards of glass slashed at his skin. Tiny pieces imbedded themselves into the top and side of his left hand. They would have struck his right too but he'd unconsciously realized something was coming at the car and had been trying to swerve away from it. His left cheek took the worst of it, shredded by the flying shards.

Rigdon's foot smashed the brakes to the floor even as the car was shoved off its course by the impact. The car spun in a half circle knocking the Sasquatch from its feet. Bleeding and stunned, Rigdon shook his head, trying to clear it. He stole a glance over at Clarkson in the passenger seat. The senior deputy was already free of his seatbelt and diving from the car. Rigdon heard Clarkson's AR booming. His head was still spinning. He just couldn't get it together. Seconds later, Clarkson leaned back into the car.

"Come on, Rigdon!" Clarkson snarled. "Get your ass moving!"

Releasing his own seatbelt, Rigdon tried to open his door, flinching in pain as he threw his weight onto it only to have it not open. His shoulder gave more than the crunched in door did, dislocating in its socket. Rigdon wailed in fresh pain. Feeling trapped, he hurled himself in the other direction, scrambling towards the passenger side door. Clarkson had already moved out of his way by the time he reached it. Rigdon half lunged, half fell out of the patrol car onto the asphalt of the road. The flesh of his palms were painful, scraped by its rough surface, leaving red where they had made contact as Rigdon rose to his feet.

"They're all around us!" Clarkson yelled, letting loose a burst of fire from his AR.

Rigdon didn't have a clue what Clarkson thought he could do about it. His left arm hung limply at his side, useless, and the only weapon he had was the Glock holstered on his hip. Nonetheless, Rigdon drew the pistol.

An inhuman howl caused Rigdon's head to jerk around. A Sasquatch on the other side of the patrol car was sprinting towards them. Rigdon raised his Glock but there was no need. Clarkson's AR was already blazing. Dozens of rounds tore at and into the monster. Rigdon watched as the Sasquatch slowed, staggering, and then collapsed to its knees. Clarkson finished up with a three round burst to its forehead, sending the Sasquatch back to whatever hell it had crawled out of.

"Damn it! That was it!" Clarkson spat. "I'm out!"

The senior deputy threw away his AR and

swung open the rear passenger side door of the patrol car to get at the shotgun lying on it. He snatched up the weapon, working its pump, to chamber a round.

Rigdon finally took a real look around and realized just how deep in it the two of them were. Their car was trashed and the only other vehicle within sight was a pick up truck that lay on its side. Part of a dead man's body, the lower half with purple, red slicked entrails spilling out of it, was on the road next to it. There was nothing they could use to escape. All they could do was either hold their ground and try to keep the beasts at bay or make a run for it on foot. He figured that was Clarkson's call. So far, the senior deputy had been managing to kill anything that emerged from the woods but now with his AR empty. . . their position had gone from tenuous to flat out suicidal.

"Crap! That shoulder of yours looks bad," Clarkson scowled. "Think you can make it if we run?"

"It's my shoulder not my fragging legs," Rigdon frowned. "But where the hell are you planning on running to?"

"Hell if I know," Clarkson shrugged.

"Up the road then?" Rigdon asked.

"As good a plan as any," Clarkson nodded as another Sasquatch came into sight. It was charging up the road from behind the patrol car.

Rigdon aimed for the Sasquatch's head. His Glock cracked four times in rapid succession. His first shot missed. The second and third both found their target, one striking the beast's nose with the sound of crunching bone, and the other reducing its right eye to an exploding glop of red pulp and gore. His fourth merely grazed the Sasquatch's right ear. They weren't enough to stop the barreling giant. Clarkson's 12 gauge was though. He stepped in front of Rigdon, his shotgun booming, as he put a round into the Sasquatch's stomach, opening it up. Guts and blood were blown outward as the heavy slug ripped its way inside the monster. Working the pump of his shotgun with the speed of the professional that he was, Clarkson fired a second time. The blast removed a chunk of meat and hair from the Sasquatch's shoulder and spun the beast about. It dropped with a loud thud onto the road, twitching, strands of its intestines being thrashed around like angry snakes. Clarkson didn't waste a third round on the Sasquatch.

"Let's move before another shows itself," Clarkson yelled and started up the road.

His shoulder hurt like hell with each jarring step but Rigdon managed to stay right behind the senior deputy. All around them, the roars and shrieks of God only knew how many Sasquatches rang out in the night. Rigdon thought he could see several sets of burning yellow eyes among the trees watching them but wasn't fully sure if they were real or conjured up by his frantic and frightened imagination.

Rigdon didn't know how long they had been running. It felt like forever. Each step was more pained than the last. Rigdon didn't know how much longer he could keep going. Clarkson was sweating and panting just as much as he was.

Clarkson skidded to a halt in front of him so suddenly that Rigdon nearly ran straight into his back.

"Oh frag me," Clarkson stammered.

A battered van sat in the middle of the road and three hulking Sasquatches had come around from behind it to block their path. Their eyes glowed a hot, feral yellow in the dimness of the moonlight.

"We are so dead," Rigdon mumbled under his breath.

Clarkson must have heard him because the senior deputy said, "Not yet we ain't. Aim for their soft bits."

The largest of the three beasts reared back its head to give a thunderous roar. The other two Sasquatches sprang forward, rushing them. Both Clarkson and Rigdon were ready for the beasts. The senior deputy's shotgun boomed. The round hammered into the face of the Sasquatch coming towards him. The creature was stopped in its tracks, clasping its hands over the mangled, bloody mess of damage the round had done.

Rigdon waited until the other Sasquatch was almost on him. His Glock cracked in rapid succession as out of desperation he targeted the beast's groin. A series of rounds pierced its testicles and the flesh of its inner thighs. The beast, likely in shock from the pain, tripped over its own feet, thudding onto the road. Rigdon ignored the pain in his shoulder hurrying to close on the downed Sasquatch. One of its hairy hands snaked out, trying to get a hold of him. Rigdon dodged the wounded creature's attempt, leaping over its extended arms, to get as close as he could before firing his pistol. Its barrel was maybe two inches from the Sasquatch's right eye. The bullet tore into the beast's head, entering its brain. The shot was enough to end it. The Sasquatch's body went limp and lay still.

Rigdon had no time to savor his victory however. The sound of Clarkson screaming spun him around. The initial Sasquatch that had come at the senior deputy was dead. He'd succeeded in stopping it but the largest of the three creatures had managed to close on him. The beast held Clarkson in its arms, squeezing the senior deputy to its chest in a bear hug. Clarkson's bones crunched loudly, breaking from the pressure of the beast's grip. Rigdon took aim at the Sasquatch's head with his Glock. When he took his shot, the Sasquatch jerked up Clarkson's crushed corpse to block the bullet coming at it.

"Frag!" Rigdon's Glock clicked empty when he tried to fire the weapon again.

The Sasquatch hurled Clarkson's body away and roared as it sprang forward. Time seemed to slow down to Rigdon as he saw the beast coming, a juggernaut of hair-covered muscle. Knowing that even if he wasn't injured, there likely wouldn't have been time to eject the Glock's spent magazine and shove another home, Rigdon ran for his life. He darted to the left and then swung about angling his path for the van hoping such a swing would throw off the monster for a couple of seconds. And every second was going to count. There was no chance of outrunning the beast. Rigdon was sure of that. His plan sucked but it was the best Rigdon could come up with on the fly. Making it around the corner of the van, Rigdon could smell the gas leaking out of its busted tank. His Glock clattered onto the road as Rigdon dug in his pocket for the lighter he knew was in there somewhere. Fingers closing around it, he yanked it out and flicked it until the lighter caught. Leaving its flame burning, Rigdon dropped the zippo into the leaking fuel as he kept running, changing his direction away from the van to towards the horizon. He heard the hulking Sasquatch come roaring around the corner of the van in his wake and then everything lit up. The van exploded, flames blossoming outward from it, debris flying. A piece of jagged metal struck Rigdon in the back, imbedding itself there. He screamed in pain from the unexpected wound as the shockwave of the explosion lifted him from the road and flung him onward through the air.

Rigdon's eyes fluttered open. He looked down the length of his body to see the tip of a jagged bit of metal from the van sticking up through the middle of his body. The intensity of the pain he was in prevented him from moving. There was more light now. The van was burning somewhere behind him. All Rigdon could do was lie there, moaning and bleeding, as a shadow fell over him. Struggling to suck in each breath he took with a sickening wheeze, Rigdon looked up at the Sasquatch towering over him. The great beast cocked its head, looking him over as the low rumble of a growl rose from its throat. Rigdon's breath caught. He coughed, blood splattering out of his mouth as his body heaved upwards. Having cleared his airway, Rigdon sucked in another breath. He was dying. The monster standing over him wasn't going to let him just lay there and bleed out though. The last thing Rigdon saw was the bottom of the

Sasquatch's foot as it came down, his head popping like an overripe melon being struck by a sledgehammer beneath it as brain matter and blood splashed all over the road.

****

The Tahoe PPV (Police Pursuit Vehicle) sped along Allen's Creek Road. A single patrol car followed in its wake. Sheriff Bernard was at the wheel of the Tahoe. The chubby kid, Brently, and the young girl, Megan were with him. Brently sat in the rear while Megan was next to Bernard in the passenger seat, her hand clutching the shotgun he had given her. Steph and the other kid, Robbie, were in the patrol car with Miller, his only remaining deputy. That last bit struck him hard as he thought it. Bernard knew it was almost certainly true though. If any of his other officers were still alive they would have shown up at the station or found a means of reaching them by now. Hell, as best Bernard could figure things, odds were every damn person in Canton was dead. It was still a difficult thing to accept.

The two vehicles were headed for Buncombe County and the city of Asheville. Bernard figured no matter how riled up and ticked off the rampaging beasts were, they wouldn't attack a city, not even one as small as Asheville. They'd stick to the rural towns in the area until content with the amount of blood that was shed and then return to the woods. Asheville was the best hope of somewhere safe in the area. They were already far away from the town of Canton and navigating the less traveled, almost forgotten route to Asheville.

The radio on the dash crackled. Bernard snatched it up as Miller spoke.

"Sir," Miller called, "I just realized what else is on this road."

As soon as Miller had spoken, he remembered too and cursed himself for being an idiot. The National Guard Base! Bernard's mind screamed. It was on this road, secluded and out of the way.

"The armory," he responded, keeping his voice a calmer than he felt.

"Yes sir," Miller confirmed. "If I remember right, we should be coming up on it soon."

As the National Guard Base came into view, Bernard slowed the Tahoe. It was clear one hell of a battle had taken place. The asphalt of the road was shattered and blown apart up ahead. It looked to be the work of a powerful RPG or something akin to one. There were several Sasquatch corpses around where the explosion had happened or rather bits of them. Bernard brought the Tahoe to a complete stop and craned his head around to look towards the base itself. The fence that ran around its perimeter was smashed to the ground, metal poles bent and broken. There were more Sasquatch bodies in that direction too but at the fence and beyond it, they weren't the only ones. Dead soldiers were everywhere.

"Damn," Miller's voice came over the radio. She was seeing the same devastation that he was. "That's crazy."

"Tell me about it," Bernard grunted back at her.

"Miller, tell Steph and that kid with you to stay in the car," Bernard ordered. "The two of us are going to check this out."

"I don't think that's a good idea, sir," Megan said.

"I didn't ask you," Bernard growled and instantly regretted it. With a heavy sigh, he turned to look at her. Megan was a tough girl who had, against all odds, survived the hell that had swept through the town that he had failed to protect tonight. She met his eyes and he was in that instant even more impressed by her. There was strength in them, hard and determined.

"You wanna know why I am stopping, right?" Bernard asked.

Megan nodded.

"That base over there. . ." Bernard started. "There could be radios or something in it that can reach someone outside of these mountains. That alone is worth stopping for. We damn well need help and you know it. And we might have some firepower from the department but the crap in there. . . it's military grade. If we run into more of those beasts," Bernard couldn't bring himself to call the things Sasquatches or whatever the hell the plural of that was, "that's sure something we can put to good use."

Bernard took a breath. "The main reason we're stopping other than the hope of getting in touch with someone outside of these mountains is that there might be a better vehicle we can get our hands on in there. Something with some armor and firepower of its own. This Tahoe ain't bad but against those things. . ." He let his voice trail off.

"But we're close to Asheville now, aren't we?" Megan pressed him.

"Not close enough," Bernard shook his head. "We've got at least another hour on these backroads before we'll reach a main one again. That's a hell of a lot of time for those things to get the drop on us out here."

Megan didn't say anything more as Bernard shoved open his door and stepped out of the PPV, closing it behind him. He opened the rear passenger door and reached inside to pick up a shotgun from the cache of weapons resting on the floorboard there. Bernard worked its pump, readying the weapon.

"You two stay in this vehicle," Bernard told Megan and the chuddy kid, Brently. "If things go south, you slide over behind the wheel and get out of here. You got that?"

"Yes sir," Megan nodded.

Bernard closed the rear door and walked to meet up with Miller who was already coming his way. She looked ready for war. An AR1-15 with a drum magazine was in her hands. There was a shotgun like his own strapped to her back and a pistol holstered on each of her hips. A few flash bangs and a tear gas grenade dangled from her belt too. A tactical armor vest covered her chest. Bernard smirked at the sight of it. It wasn't as if the monsters were going to be shooting back at them but he couldn't blame Miller for putting it on. The stuff might just soften a blow from one of those beasts and it would certainly offer at least some protection from their claws.

"You sure about this?" Miller frowned.

He nodded. "I got point."

Bernard started walking into the base through the remnants of its crumpled outer fence. Miller fell in behind him, staying more than a few steps behind. The battle at the base had to have really been a hell of a thing, Bernard reckoned. The smell of death and smoke filled the night air. He couldn't see any fires that were still actively burning. There were two smashed up trucks that appeared to have been on their way out of the base when the attack started. They were completely trashed, engine blocks smashed in, doors ripped off, and worse.

"God have mercy," he heard Miller mutter behind him.

"The big guy didn't have anything to do with this," Bernard assured her. "These bastards were caught unprepared and flat out massacred. They didn't have a fragging prayer."

The bodies of the dead soldiers were strewn all over the area behind the fence's entrance and especially around the trucks where they had tried to make a stand. Bernard shook his head at the sight, nostrils crinkling at the smell of so much blood and guts.

"Come on," Bernard barked, heading onward towards the main building in the center of the base. It was dark without a single light he could see inside it. Its shattered glass front doors showed that the beasts hadn't stopped their rampage outside.

"They hit the garages too," Miller told him, nodding in the direction of a structure to their right.

Bernard stopped ten yards or so short of the entrance to the main building. Miller moved to stand at his side.

"How do you want to handle this?" she asked. "Those things could still be in there."

"I don't think hiding in the shadows is their

style," Bernard huffed.

Miller shrugged. "I don't know, sir. You have to think about how long they've been hiding out there in the woods without anyone ever knowing for sure if they were even real or not until now."

Bernard laughed despite himself. "Can't argue that."

Without warning, a hulking, hairy beast came bursting out of the building. Its black lips twisted in a feral snarl and yellow eyes blazing, the thing moved with seemingly impossible speed.

"Miller!" Bernard shouted.

He and Miller opened fire together. His shotgun thundered as Miller's AR-15 chattered furiously. The huge Sasquatch staggered from the barrage of hot lead they poured into it. Miller had put dozens of rounds into its chest by the time Bernard's second shotgun blast knocked the Sasquatch from its feet.

Miller was staring at the Sasquatch and the pool of red leaking out around its crumpled form as numerous howls and shrieks rang out in the night from all around the base.

She tore her eyes away from the beast's body and looked at him. "We are so fragging screwed."

Bernard didn't yell or shout, he simply said, "Run."

And they did. Miller was ahead of him as Bernard hung back in case he needed to cover her.

****

As the howls and shrieks of the Sasquatch in the woods continued, seeming to draw closer with each passing second, Megan crawled over into the Tahoe's driver's seat.

"What the hell are you waiting for?" Brently shouted from the backseat. "Get us out of here!"

"No!" Megan snapped. "We can't just take off. The Sheriff and Deputy Miller are still in the base."

"That's what he freaking told you to do, Megan!" Brently squealed.

He lunged up, trying to get into the front with her. Megan met him with a clenched fist to the forehead that knocked Brently back onto his butt.

"Ow!" Brently wailed.

"Shut the hell up!" Megan told him. "I need to think!"

The patrol car was still behind the Tahoe. She saw its interior light come on as someone opened its rear driver's side door and got out. It was Robbie. He came running over and tugged on the passenger side door. She had locked it before climbing over to take Sheriff Bernard's seat in the Tahoe. Megan released the lock.

Robbie, yanking the door open, leaped inside the Tahoe, and slammed it shut behind him.

"Megan!" Robbie locked eyes with her. "We have to get out of here now."

"What?" Megan eyed him. "We can't just leave the Sheriff. We owe him our lives."

"If we don't get moving right now, we never will and you know it," Robbie told her. "Think about it. You heard the Sasquatch out there and know how many of them there must be."

Megan had never seen Robbie so freaked out before. Usually, he was the cool headed member of their group of friends. She was torn, not wanting to abandon the sheriff but also knowing deep down that Robbie was right. Tears welling up in her eyes, Megan slammed the Tahoe's gas pedal to the floor. The Tahoe shot forward down Allen's Creek Road.

Steph watched as the Tahoe sped away. She cursed herself for letting Robbie out of the car but then what was she supposed to do, shoot him? Steph could have. Her knuckles were white from the tightness of the grip she held her shotgun in.

"Damn it," she frowned, tears sliding down the curves of her cheeks. She was alone again just like in the department before the others had shown up. There was no way in hell she was getting out of the car to go looking for Sheriff Bernard and Miller. Steph's heart was pounding so hard it felt like it was going to explode out of her chest. Realizing she was sobbing, Steph forced herself to take a deep breath and tried to get control of her emotions. Then she saw them coming.

Sheriff Bernard cleared the crumpled mess of the base's fence with Deputy Miller on his heels. She saw the startled expression on Bernard's face at the Tahoe being gone. Then, Steph flung her door open.

"Get the hell in here!" she yelled at them.

Sheriff Bernard sprinted for the driver's side of the patrol car while Miller got in behind Steph. As Steph turned to Miller, her breath caught in her lungs and her eyes bugged. Through the rear window, past Miller, Steph saw the beasts coming out of the woods. There were nearly half a dozen of the creatures, all at least eight feet tall and all snarling, yellow eyes burning with rage in the darkness.

The slamming of the driver's door snapped Steph out of her terror induced shock. Sheriff Bernard cranked the patrol car and floored the gas. The car lurched forward. . . straight into a Sasquatch that was charging towards it. Metal crunched as the car's hood folded up and the forward windshield smashed. All of them were flung forward in their seats. Steph, who had partially turned towards the sheriff, felt her ribs strike the dashboard. She gave a yelp of pain.

Miller was slammed into the back of Steph's seat while Sheriff Bernard's forehead smacked down into the steering wheel in front of him.

Steph could see that Sheriff Bernard had been knocked unconscious. Thankfully, the beast the car had rammed into was in no shape to come at them. The thing was sprawled out on the road with its guts spilling out of its ruptured stomach.

"You okay?" Miller shouted from the back seat.

"Yeah," Steph lied, knowing that at least one of her ribs had been broken when she hit the dash. It hurt to breathe.

"Stay in the car," Miller ordered, leaping out of the back with her AR-15 in hand.

Steph knew that staying in the patrol car wasn't going to save her. With Sheriff Bernard unconscious, Miller was stepping up and playing the part of the hero by getting out to engage the Sasquatch that were beginning to surround the vehicle.

Miller's AR-15 roared, peppering the body of the beast she aimed for with bloody wounds. The deputy didn't see the Sasquatch approaching from her flank until it was too late. Oversized, hairy hands took hold of her rifle, bending the weapon as it was ripped away from Miller's grasp. Miller went for the pistol holstered on her right hip but the Sasquatch was faster. It grabbed hold of her head and smashed it into the side of the patrol car. Gore splashed everywhere as Miller's skull was flattened like a pancake between the beast's palm and the metal there.

Steph flinched in her seat, jerking her head around at the sound of the driver's side door being wrenched from the car. The Sasquatch that had torn it free flung the door away. It leaned into the vehicle, taking hold of Sheriff Bernard. Steph screamed as the beast heaved his body out from the car and dropped it onto the road. The Sasquatch started stomping on the sheriff, grunting with each downward thrust of the foot it was using. Steph knew her only hope was to run.

Flinging her door open, Steph bolted from the patrol car, shotgun falling from her hands in the process. It clattered onto the road, nearly tripping her. Steph ducked as the clawed hand of the beast that had ended Miller's life swung outward, swiping through the air above her head. Jerking back upright, Steph ran like hell away from the car and the Sasquatch, heading towards the crumpled fence of the base. If she could just get inside one of the base's buildings, maybe, just maybe there would be a place to escape the monsters and hide.

Before Steph had even managed to reach the fence, a hair-covered fist hammered into her back. Bones cracked and gave way beneath the sheer brute force of its impact. The blow knocked Steph from her feet and sent her bouncing along the asphalt. Steph came to rest, sprawled out on the ground, white, jagged pieces of her ribs sticking outward through the red soaked cloth of the shirt she wore. Things shifted and hurt inside as she tried to get up and failed, the pain nearly causing her to pass out. An oversized, bestial hand closed around her neck, lifting Steph up. Legs kicking and thrashing in the air, Steph's fingernails dug into the arm of the Sasquatch holding her. Steph fought with everything she had left in her to get free but it was all in vain. The Sasquatch wrenched up further and to the right before smashing her down. Steph died instantly, skull fractured and most of her other bones shattered against the road.

****

Megan was barely able to handle the Tahoe on the curvy backroad. She had a license but only just and without a car of her own, there hadn't been a lot of practice. Aching inside from the guilt of leaving the Sheriff behind, Megan felt sick. Robbie had taken her shotgun. Megan was okay with that for the time being. Someone needed to be ready to deal with the Sasquatch if they attacked the Tahoe while it was moving.

Brently leaned over and threw up all over the backseat. The smell of it was sick and horrid.

"Damn, man," Robbie chided him. "What the hell? Weren't things bad enough already?"

"Sorry," Brently said weakly, still looking green tinged and not well. "I couldn't help it."

"Forget it," Megan told them both.

The Tahoe skidded around a sharp twist in the road, tires squealing in protest. It made the turn though. Megan fought with the wheel to get the big vehicle righted and back onto a straight course.

The boys were quiet.

"Look, Megan, there was no other hope of us getting out of there. . ." Robbie started.

"I am so not having that conversation with you right now," she snarled, glancing over at him.

"Hey!" Brently thumped the back of the driver's seat. "What's that up there?"

Megan yelped, hitting the Tahoe's brakes. Ahead was the biggest roadblock she'd ever seen. There was a pile of sand bags that stretched completely across the roadway. Behind it were army soldiers, real army, not more guardsmen like those who had been slaughtered. There were two Jeeps, each with a giant machine gun mounted in its rear.

"Those are .50 calibers," Robbie swallowed loudly.

A voice boosted by a loudspeaker barked, "Get out of the car with your hands up!"

Megan and Robbie opened their doors stepping out, hands held above their heads. Two super bright spotlights turned on, their light stinging Megan's eyes and nearly blinding her.

"Fragging A man!" someone behind the roadblock exclaimed. "They're just kids!"

But the amplified voice boomed again. "The person in the back, too!"

"Come on, Brently. Get out here!" Robbie urged.

As Brently opened the rear passenger side door, all hell broke loose. In front of them, the soldiers all started yelling and freaking out, guns being aimed in their direction. Behind them, the night was filled with bestial roars and fierce snarls. Megan looked over her shoulder to see a dozen or more Sasquatch sprinting towards the road block.

"Get down!" someone shouted and Megan dropped flat to the road. Megan didn't stay where she was though. Crawling on her belly as fast as she could, Megan dragged herself towards the roadblock.

She heard a shotgun thunder and knew it had to be Robbie. The soldiers she'd seen were all armed with wicked looking rifles. The cacophony of automatic fire was deafening. The two .50 caliber machine guns added to the noise of the small arms fire of the soldiers. The many roars from the Sasquatch became shrieks and wails. Megan couldn't risk looking back though. She needed to reach the barricade as quickly as possible.

She sucked in a terrified breath as a hairy foot thudded down onto the pavement near her face. The beast it belonged to didn't even notice her as it ran onward, charging headlong into the barrage of fire being put out by the soldiers behind the barricade.

Megan heard men screaming as some of the beasts reached the barricade. Stopping where she was, Megan kept as still as she could. The safety of being with the soldiers didn't seem so safe anymore.

The air stunk of gun smoke, blood, and entrails, gagging her. As she lay there, silent tears ran from Megan's eyes. And then as fast as it all started, it was over. The gunfire of the soldiers had fallen quiet along with their screams. The roars of the beasts were quieter too, fewer in number and growing more distant with each passing heartbeat.

They broke through, Megan thought.

Soon, everything was completely silent except for soft drips of blood splattering onto the asphalt. Megan lay there until her heart stopped fluttering and she was as sure as possible that none of the Sasquatch were still around. Slowly, Megan rose to her feet, staggering first towards the barricade then turning to look around. There were corpses everywhere, Sasquatch shredded and pulped by high powered rounds and soldiers crushed or torn apart by clawed hands.

Seeing that there really were no Sasquatch, at least that were still breathing, about to threaten her, Megan rushed to check on Robbie and Brently. She saw Brently first. His chubby body had been cut apart by machine gun fire. Its top half lay on the road near the open rear door of the Tahoe. She couldn't see the lower half and didn't put effort into looking for it.

Robbie was just as dead. It hadn't been friendly fire that killed him but one of the beasts. He lay on his back, rib cage cracked open and spread apart, half of his face slashed away by a swipe of sharp claws.

Something snapped in Megan. All her fear and hurt morphed into a deep, seething hatred. Cheeks flushed with rage, she ran to the line of sand bags and jumped over them. She snatched up the rifle of the closest dead soldier and popped its magazine to check for ammo then slammed it back into the weapon. Megan went about looting the dead for more ammo and weapons. When she was finally content, Megan knew she was going to need a vehicle. The Tahoe had been shot to hell during the battle and was useless.

Depositing her loot into the rear of the closest Jeep, Megan dragged a soldier's corpse out of it. The man's corpse flopped onto the road. The Sasquatch were going to pay for everything they'd done tonight. That was the promise Megan made herself. The town where she had grown up was no more and everyone she knew was dead.

The Sasquatch were heading out into the rest of the Western North Carolina now and by God, she was going after them. She cranked up the Jeep's engine as the first dim rays of the early dawn filled the sky above her and then stomped a foot down on the gas. Megan whirled the Jeep around and sped off in the direction of Asheville and the battle she knew lay ahead. She was going after the beasts. . .and hell followed with her.

END

Author Bio

Eric S Brown is the author of numerous book series including the Bigfoot War series, The Psi-Mechs Inc. series, the Kaiju Apocalypse series (with Jason Cordova), the Crypto-Squad series (with Jason Brannon), the Homeworld series (With Tony Faville and Jason Cordova), the Jack Bunny Bam series, and the A Pack of Wolves series. Some of his stand alone books include War of the Worlds plus Blood Guts and Zombies, Casper Alamo (with Jason Brannon), Sasquatch Island, Day of the Sasquatch, Bigfoot, Crashed, World War of the Dead, Last Stand in a Dead Land, Sasquatch Lake, Kaiju Armageddon, Megalodon, Megalodon Apocalypse, Kraken, Alien Battalion, The Last Fleet, and From the Snow They Came to name only a few. His short fiction has been published hundreds of times in the small press in beyond including markets like the Onward Drake and Black Tide Rising anthologies from Baen Books, the Grantville Gazette, the SNAFU Military horror anthology series, and Walmart World magazine. He has done the novelizations for such films as Boggy Creek: The Legend is True (Studio 3 Entertainment) and The Bloody Rage of Bigfoot (Great Lake films). The first book of his Bigfoot

War series was adapted into a feature film by Origin Releasing in 2014. Werewolf Massacre at Hell's Gate was the second of his books to be adapted into film in 2015. Major Japanese publisher, Takeshobo, bought the reprint rights to his Kaiju Apocalypse series (with Jason Cordova) and the mass market, Japanese language version was released in late 2017. Ring of Fire Press has released a collected edition of his Monster Society stories (set in the New York Times Best-selling world of Eric Flint's 1632). In addition to his fiction, Eric also writes an award-winning comic book news column entitled "Comics in a Flash" as well a pop culture column for Altered Reality Magazine. Eric lives in North Carolina with his wife and two children where he continues to write tales of the hungry dead, blazing guns, and the things that lurk in the woods.

Check out other great

Cryptid Novels!

P.K. Hawkins

THE CRYPTID FILES

Fresh out of the academy with top marks, Agent Bradley Tennyson is expecting to have the pick of cases and investigations throughout the country. So he's shocked when instead he is assigned as the new partner to "The Crag," an agent well past his prime. He thinks the assignment is a punishment. It's anything but.Agent George Crag has been doing this job for far longer than most, and he knows what skeletons his bosses have in the closet and where the bodies are buried. He has pretty much free reign to pick his cases, and he knows exactly which one he wants to use to break in his new young partner: the disappearance and murder of a couple of college kids in a remote mountain town.Tennyson doesn't realize it, but Crag is about to introduce him to a world he never believed existed: The Cryptid Files, a world of strange monsters roaming in the night. Because these murders have been going on for a long time, and evidence is mounting that the murderer may just in fact be the legendary Bigfoot.

Gerry Griffiths

DOWN FROM
BEAST MOUNTAIN

A beast with a grudge has come down from the mountain to terrorize the townsfolk of Porterville. The once sleepy town is suddenly wide awake. Sheriff Abel McGuire and game warden Grant Tanner frantically investigate one brutal slaying after another as they follow the blood trail they hope will eventually lead to the monstrous killer. But they better hurry and stop the carnage before the census taker has to come out and change the population sign on the edge of town to ZERO.

Check out other great
Cryptid Novels!

J.H. Moncrieff
RETURN TO DYATLOV PASS

In 1959, nine Russian students set off on a skiing expedition in the Ural Mountains. Their mutilated bodies were discovered weeks later. Their bizarre and unexplained deaths are one of the most enduring true mysteries of our time. Nearly sixty years later, podcast host Nat McPherson ventures into the same mountains with her team, determined to finally solve the mystery of the Dyatlov Pass incident. Her plans are thwarted on the first night, when two trackers from her group are brutally slaughtered. The team's guide, a superstitious man from a neighboring village, blames the killings on yetis, but no one believes him. As members of Nat's team die one by one, she must figure out if there's a murderer in their midst—or something even worse—before history repeats itself and her group becomes another casualty of the infamous Dead Mountain.

Gerry Griffiths
CRYPTID ZOO

As a child, rare and unusual animals, especially cryptid creatures, always fascinated Carter Wilde. Now that he's an eccentric billionaire and runs the largest conglomerate of high-tech companies all over the world, he can finally achieve his wildest dream of building the most incredible theme park ever conceived on the planet... CRYPTID ZOO. Even though there have been apparent problems with the project, Wilde still decides to send some of his marketing employees and their families on a forced vacation to assess the theme park in preparation for Opening Day. Nick Wells and his family are some of those chosen and are about to embark on what will become the most terror-filled weekend of their lives—praying they survive. STEP RIGHT UP AND GET YOUR FREE PASS... TO CRYPTID ZOO

SEVEREDPRESS

Check out other great

Cryptid Novels!

Hunter Shea

LOCH NESS REVENGE

Deep in the murky waters of Loch Ness, the creature known as Nessie has returned. Twins Natalie and Austin McQueen watched in horror as their parents were devoured by the world's most infamous lake monster. Two decades later, it's their turn to hunt the legend. But what lurks in the Loch is not what they expected. Nessie is devouring everything in and around the Loch, and it's not alone. Hell has come to the Scottish Highlands. In a fierce battle between man and monster, the world may never be the same. Praise for THEY RISE : "Outrageous, balls to the wall...made me yearn for 3D glasses and a tub of popcorn, extra butter!" – The Eyes of Madness "A fast-paced, gore-heavy splatter fest of sharksploitation." The Werd "A rocket paced horror story. I enjoyed the hell out of this book." Shotgun Logic Reviews

C.G. Mosley

BAKER COUNTY BIGFOOT CHRONICLE

Marie Bledsoe only wants her missing brother Kurt back. She'll stop at nothing to make it happen and, with the help of Kurt's friend Tony, along with Sheriff Ray Cochran, Marie embarks on a terrifying journey deep into the belly of the mysterious Walker Laboratory to find him. However, what she and her companions find lurking in the laboratory basement is beyond comprehension. There are cryptids from the forest being held captive there and something...else. Enjoy this suspenseful tale from the mind of C.G. Mosley, author of Wood Ape. Welcome back to Baker County, a place where monsters do lurk in the night!

Made in the USA
Las Vegas, NV
06 December 2022

61285782R00079